MANY SHADES OF HER

A TRUE HOLLYWOOD STORY

JOHN ALAN ANDREWS

#1 INTERNATIONAL BESTSELLING AUTHOR

MANY SHADES OF HER

Copyright © 2025 by John A. Andrews.

All rights reserved. The publisher must secure written permission to use or reproduce any part of this book except for brief quotations in critical reviews or articles.

Published in the U.S.A. by

Books That Will Enhance Your Life™

A L I - Andrews Leadership International
www.JohnAAndrews.com

Cover Design: John A. Andrews

Cover Graphic Designer: A L I

Cover Photo: Somer Ray

Edited by: A L I

ISBN: **9798305954500**

MANY SHADES OF HER

TABLE OF CONTENTS

CHAPTER ONE...4
CHAPTER TWO...7
CHAPTER THREE...9
CHAPTER FOUR...13
CHAPTER FIVE...19
CHAPTER SIX..24
CHAPTER SEVEN..33
CHAPTER EIGHT..36
CHAPTER NINE...44
CHAPTER TEN..47
CHAPTER ELEVEN...49
CHAPTER TWELVE...52
CHAPTER THIRTEEN...63
CHAPTER FOURTEEN...66
CHAPTER FIFTEEN..70
CHAPTER SIXTEEN..73
CHAPTER SEVENTEEN..77
CHAPTER EIGHTEEN...80
CHAPTER NINETEEN...84
CHAPTER TWENTY...87
CHAPTER TWENTY-ONE...92
CHAPTER TWENTY-TWO...95
CHAPTER TWENTY-THREE...98
CHAPTER TWENTY-FOUR...102
CHAPTER TWENTY-FIVE...105
CHAPTER TWENTY-SIX..108
CHAPTER TWENTY-SEVEN..111
CHAPTER TWENTY-EIGHT..115

CHAPTER ONE

Will Mansfield was a very ambitious businessman who had gone through a divorce and tried to make a colossal comeback in Hollywood. He also owned a modeling agency in Studio City, California, and vowed to catch up with Ford and Elite Models.

At the same time, Steve Barnes, aka Steve, an aspiring actor and businessman, was in the honeymoon stage of a much-contested divorce.

MANY SHADES OF HER

Through a mutual friend, Bob Constantine, a seasoned commercial actor, Steve Barnes was introduced to Will Mansfield on a three-way cell phone call.
A few days later, Steve met with Will over dinner. Anything to get Steve Barnes back on his feet seemed plausible. Steve Barnes was in a pickle, losing his dwelling and much more after his hotly contested divorce settlement.
Will Mansfield, also a recent divorcee, talked Steve into a roommate scenario so they could cut costs and build the modeling business. The duo, both opportunists, instantly bonded like two peas in a pod and embarked on the hustle.
The small dwelling hugging the main street Ventura Boulevard in Studio City had no bedroom, just a living room—a small room that Will Mansfield used as his office and fixtured with a shower and an adjacent restroom. The living room featured a patterned green couch on which Will slept, a glass-top center table, and a few table chairs. Steve Barnes slept on the living room floor, aided by two comforters and a pillow. Steve soon got accustomed to these lyrics:
Cold ground was my bed last night, but I had my pillow...
They open for business daily during the day, using that glass center table to promote Zed cards and

industry magazines. At night, they use the lounge to sleep. This underground modeling agency, chasing Ford and Elite, attracted some of Hollywood's finest models.

The duo kept the Boutique Agency neat and clean to their advantage.

Oblivious to their growing client roster, Will Mansfield and Steve Barnes use the office as their habitat. Mansfield nursed a part-time day job as an editor in the entertainment industry. Steve ran the agency on weekdays, and Will Mansfield assisted full-time on weekends.

Steve Barnes, an opportunist and problem solver focused on rebounding, sharpened his skills in anticipation of the next opportunity. Right after 911, which crushed most industries, Will Mansfield was shattered and brought a lethargic work ethic to the representation game.

CHAPTER TWO

Subsequently, Steve Barnes, seeing the writing on the wall, cut Will Mansfield loose and opened an agency in the heart of Hollywood. Zed cards flooded the model's wall. Like a man on assignment, Steve Barnes built this Boutique Modeling Agency to a roster of over 35 models in less than six months.

Business boomed, and Steve Barnes was able to upgrade his "no car status" to a used Mazda 626. He even went back to acting classes, honing his craft while working solo from 9 to 5 at his modeling agency, which grew considerably in roster size.

This one-man show motivated him, and he hit the ground running. The payoff also enabled him to afford basketball lessons for his three sons, 5, 3, and 2 years old.

Barnes interviewed a handsome male model; let's call him Tom. He was of GQ quality. Tom found out about Steve Barnes' on the agency's website and solicited an interview. Steve, very impressed by Tom, immediately brought him on board.

Tom was tall and well-built, much like a lady's magnet. Barnes immediately put Tom to work. As the money flowed in, Tom became desperate for an apartment in that Hollywood neighborhood, and Steve Barnes, eager to step up his living conditions, shared those same aspirations.

So, in less than one week, their dream came true; they acquired their dream suite, which is a five-minute walk from the agency.

This two-bedroom, two-bath suite, with a full kitchen and balcony, was a charm for the two alpha males. It was also equipped with a swimming pool, sauna, and gym on the ground floor. Guests stopped by and were hesitant to leave.

CHAPTER THREE

It was mid-morning on a beautiful spring day in 2001. After scouting tirelessly one week prior, Steve Barnes sat in his Hollywood office, eagerly waiting for his phone to ring. Seated at this office desk, he had the routine down pat. In his mind, he heard Bling! Bling! – regaining his presence of mind, he realized it was just a figment of his imagination. So, he returned to his inner self.

MANY SHADES OF HER

Was this custom about to lapse? Did he just get jinxed? He imagined as if he stared at the agency's logo on the wall. To deflect from thinking about a possible void in his morning ritual, he reminded himself that he was involved in the emblem's creative process, which reminded him he was *numero uno* – before the phone rang.

The almost empty cup displaying a Starbucks logo lay hoisted amongst stacks of photographs on his desk. He took a swig of the coffee and reached into the desk's top drawer. From there, he retrieved his day planner and perused through the more than one dozen appointments he had scheduled the night before.

For some reason, the phone still didn't ring as he anticipated. Was it malfunctioning? Steve Barnes reasoned. That thought raced through his frazzled mind as he stared intensely at the pitched-black cordless phone.

It was customary for prospective models to consistently call during those early morning hours, during or right after Steve Barnes' meditational interlude. He once again reminded himself of this occurrence as time elapsed. He stood up from his desk and looked at himself in the mirror, wishing it was full length after the first glance. Being six feet,

MANY SHADES OF HER

four inches tall and possessing a model's physique, he wanted to see himself as tall and erect.

Just a few days prior, he had broken in some new Gillette razors, which gave his head and face the neatest, cleanest shave he had ever experienced. His scalp glittered so much the mirror reflected Strictly Business. His denim blue jeans jacket and matching slacks were fresh from the cleaners, giving him that crisp look. They complimented his red and white Nike sneakers and balanced his white polo shirt with a red and black motif. He tried on his Prada glasses to complete it. Steve was so acclimated to his comfy look. He would have worn a suit and tie for these business appointments in his hometown of New York. Dressing for success was ingrained in his psyche, but this was LA, where the feeling was laid-back.

Barnes glanced at the clock on the wall, noticing his first appointment of the day was moments away. Let's call her, as he used the pseudonym EVE. She had inquiringly called a week ago, stating that she was new to Los Angeles from Chicago and interviewing with several modeling agencies looking for the right fit.

Eve claimed she was also interested in talking with Ford and Elite Models. Steve perused and liked the few pictures she sent him to whet his appetite. He had heard those stories about his two competitors before and dealt with many tardy talents who skipped auditions regularly. He had to see it for himself. So, momentarily, he thought she'd be just another bad apple in that Hollywood bunch.

During the waiting period, he reviewed her digital online pictures again. Potentially, Eve was more than he envisioned. Her facial stats included bluish-green eyes, a Blunt hairstyle, a fair-tanned complexion, and thick protruding lips accented by raised cheeks. He saw colossal marketability in her photographs. Barnes grabbed another sip of that now running-cold Starbucks brew, which refreshed as if he'd just received an adrenaline shot.

Glancing at the model's wall, he noticed a few "Zed" cards out of place. So, he immediately walked over and proceeded to arrange his wall neatly. With a copy of his day's itinerary on the desk behind him, he noticed Eve's contact number was omitted from the submission.

Mildred, his part-time Asian assistant, indeed dropped the ball. Barnes affixed the application to a clipboard and meandered across to his desk.

CHAPTER FOUR

By then, Steve's wish came true; the phone rang just like it always did after one of his meditational sessions, except this call was somewhat delayed. Could it be a potential model calling to set up an interview? Could it be his first appointment, EVE? Those thoughts permeated his "get-ready-for-a-great Monday morning" rationale.

He enthusiastically reached for the black cordless phone and answered on the second ring.
"Good morning! This is Steven Barnes,"
He said.

The voice on the other end replied:
"Good Morning! It is a great morning indeed. My name is Eve. I have a 10:30 appointment. I'm calling to inform you that I'm outside feeding the parking meter. I will be there in a few minutes."
"See you soon; we're located on the second floor, first door to the right."
Steven replied. He then picked up that empty coffee cup and quickly dumped it in the trash can beside his desk. He tidied up some more. Simultaneously, the buzzer sounded, to which he responded promptly by pressing the button on the cordless phone, which allowed her access through the front door. Parking took a while, he thought.
Steven heard footsteps coming up the stairs One, Two, One, Two. It was One, Two. Then it hit the corridor. The rhythm of the strides told him that Eve was equipped with runway experience. As the sensitivity in his ear increased, silence prevailed. Subsequently, a chatter erupted between two women. Steven Barnes was trying to make sense of their audible chattering, to no avail.

MANY SHADES OF HER

Seconds later, the door buzzer sounded, and the varied footsteps stopped. In a mad rush towards the door, Steven Barnes knocked over a stack of Zed cards, which lay on the edge of his desk. He scooped them up, re-organized the deck, and laid them back on the desk. He composed himself from the mishap and moseyed towards the door.

Steven opened the door, and two women entered. He knew which one was EVE. That was a given. Her supporting cast, he didn't. He focused on Eve, sporting a deeper tan than he'd seen in her photos. Eve was attired in a tight-fitting, low-necked, light red long-sleeved sweater. Her tight blue jeans grabbed her curvaceous hips and her long legs like they were stitched onto her body.

Her accompaniment introduced herself as Samantha. She would no doubt be suited for print work versus doing the catwalk based on her physique. She swaggered strong features like a tough cop on the beat. Steven felt as if he had captured two birds with one stone. Intonating if she wanted to be on his roster, that would be a challenge. He wasn't looking for additional plus-size models now; the two already in his camp, Esther and Bre, were enough. He glanced up at his wall to validate.

Meanwhile, Samantha, like a rookie cop, was sizing up Steven without even making eye contact. In the meantime, he engaged himself and vice versa. Samantha looked like she could be Eve's mother if her dad had a much lighter complexion. Eve was mixed with some blackness but was more vanilla than chocolate. Something was odd, though; they didn't seem to belong genetically. Before Steven could get down to the business at hand, Eve apologetically exclaimed:

"I'm sorry for the delay. Parking is a bitch in this neighborhood, huh?"

"Sometimes."

Remarked, Steven.

At this point, he felt like the interview was gaining some legs. Steven was maintaining his business posture as much as he could. He didn't want to overpromise and underdeliver, so he offered Samantha an application. She perused the document and said,

"Can I take it home and consider it? I'm here for Eve. I don't want to upstage her."

Eve was a total knockout, a bombshell; she knew it, Samantha knew it, and Steven knew it like he knew she had the most beautiful eyes he had ever seen – amber in color. Those bulging eyes pierced indelibly through the depths of Steven's very heart and soul. Eve's peripheral glance at him was more than a casual stare. It was that penetratingly obvious in his

MANY SHADES OF HER

purview. Her lips shone brightly as if glazed with delicious dripping raw honey. Her abs were like the 8th wonder of the world; her curvy hips, long graceful legs, and her well-proportioned juicy rack made her instantly, in his eyes, a very, very, very marketable commodity. Steven chose not to let his mind wander concerning her sensuality. His business hat remained glued to his head. After all, the casting breakdowns: if he signed her, it would undoubtedly present her with multiple casting opportunities.

They seemed very relaxed on the couch.

"What would you like to drink…? Soda Pop? "

He asked.

"We will have water,"

Eve replied.

He served them water from the fountain in paper cups and then handed Eve a fresh application with a pen attached to a clipboard. Samantha held on tightly to an extensive, black portfolio as if it were a personal object.

While Eve filled in the blanks, he politely asked Samantha to put the treasured collection in his hands. She consented, and he immediately began scanning through its pages. Steven liked what he saw, and this helped to validate her eligibility. He also sensed that EVE would fit nicely into his talent pool and that she could, without question, be the top model on his roster. Underneath his breath, he sported:

"If she had a burning desire, was willing to work, and put her beauty in his experienced coaching hands, we would make bank."

All this remained undiscovered.

MANY SHADES OF HER

CHAPTER FIVE

Eve, with her innocent look, was in her mid-twenties but looked eighteen to play younger. Her naivety, when silent, made her look like she had not been touched. On the other hand, her voice and her personality said:

"I'm very mature as they come. I am adept and can handle anything."

Most would say she had been here before in a previous life.

MANY SHADES OF HER

On the other hand, Samantha was meticulously scanning his model's wall to see how and if Eve would fit in. As Steven continued to size her up, Samantha looked like she was in her early to mid-40s and seasoned. He closed Eve's portfolio and returned it to Samantha before moving to and sitting behind his desk. Eve got up from the couch and followed him in tow with her application in hand.

Steven motioned her to a seat while he reviewed her application. He was meanwhile visualizing what he could do to unleash her full potential as a supermodel. Her eyes rolled past a portrait of him. On it was the inscription in black Sharpie ink: Steve Barnes, you are the best!!

"So, they call you Steve? How coincidental?"
Said, Eve.

"Yep. My mom cherished that name except when I got into trouble. She yelled at Steven! Samantha, feel free to watch some TV. We're almost done."

Like a P.I., Samanta fastened herself on the couch in clear view of the continued interview process. Reaching for the remote, Samantha switched on the Television.

First, Steve suggested an upcoming photoshoot to Eve to supplement her portfolio. She agreed to a weekend shoot, knowing her current photos were over a year old.

By this time, they were now joined by Samantha, as she plopped down on the vacant seat. Upon landing, she concurred:

"Elite Models said the same thing about her pictures."

Once again, that competitor's name surfaced. Steve was not going to let Eve slip through his hands. On the other hand, he refused to feel or look pressured. Even though on the inside, he had to have her, not another modeling agency. Plus, he had already done his homework on the majors – Ford and Elite. His goal was to one day have his roster compete with theirs.

"Really? They said she needs new photos?"

He questioned cunningly after letting that statement by Samantha float, then drop, and nodded yes.

At this point, Steve wished Eve answered on her behalf. He had to get some control out of Samantha's hands.

"Samantha, I am booked up with photoshoots, but I might be able to call in some favors if you took up my offer,"

Steve reassured.

Samantha smiled while looking at Eve, who smiled as she looked into his hopeful eyes. He then reached for and glanced through his calendar. Scanning through a list of upcoming photoshoots for that month, he noticed that Mike and John, the two photographers he employed, were all booked up. Even so, he felt obliged to accommodate. So, he got on the phone immediately and called John. It went straight to voice mail.

He called Mike and got him.

"Mike, this is Steven Barnes. I need some supplemental photos of a new model ASAP. Could we make this happen this weekend?"

Mike responded,

"You have my schedule, and it's busy, but I can do it if I do a double camera. It's the same location and a different backdrop, and it's a deal."

"Mike, you are awesome! See if you can wrap her early,"

Steve persuaded.

"Was this perfect timing? Mike had never done this for me before. He said, "No, can do," when I asked him a month ago to give me some pickup shots on Esther."

He noticed Eve's comfort level increase.

"That worked out like I thought it would."

Said Steve.

They concluded the interview with wardrobe choices. Eve got up to leave. She stuck out her hand and shook Steve's. His hand was sweaty from a sudden rush through his body. She shook it very

MANY SHADES OF HER

firmly and smartly, then cunningly turned around, displaying her well-bred backside view of blessing. Then, with her hips shaking each stride, she bid her goodbye. Her smiling, shiny lips and long, bouncy hair swerved as she left the room. Samantha smiled at him, chuckled, and followed her lead.

Eventually, Steve composed himself after that goodbye episode and saw her evolving as a pillar of the organization. Elite Models was not going to have a signing chance at her.

He perused several magazines, acquiring tear sheet after tear sheet. Preparing himself for her following interview was now taking center stage.

CHAPTER SIX

On the following Friday morning, Steve had several appointments on his plate. He was hoping that some of the other models would run into Eve. She had so much zest and zeal in her swagger. With her potential, Steve envisioned, things around here could get competitive. The battle of the chicks would ensue. Other models on his roster would have to step up to the plate. They were

MANY SHADES OF HER

going to have to bring it if they wanted to vie with Eve.

He saw an evolution if Eve got on board and met expectations.

Esther and Annabelle, two of his models, had dropped by earlier that morning. Like the early morning incoming phone calls, their visit was serendipitous or, as some may call it, well-timed. While both models lingered, he busily organized tear sheets for Eve's folder.

At one point, Esther looked concerned about some of the looks Steve was organizing. He detected Esther's concern and invited her to his desk. He began reviewing pictures taken at her latest photoshoot. Meanwhile, Annabelle sat on the couch reading a copy of Instyle Magazine while waiting her turn.

In the interim, the door buzzer sounded.

Outside, multiple visitors gathered. The buzzer rang more than usual on any given morning. Soon, numerous footsteps were heard coming up the stairs. He answered the door and was greeted by multiple walk-ins. To say the least, he was slammed, with Eve's appointment pending. He provided handouts to the walk-ins and suggested they set up an appointment if necessary. Esther departed with the crowd. Looking out his office window, Steve

MANY SHADES OF HER

could see the morning traffic on Hollywood Boulevard from bumper to bumper. He noticed his company's name nestled in with the other five offices on the building's marquee. Also, because of the building's location right in the heart of Hollywood, Steve attracted several walk-ins, but mostly during late afternoon hours. As Steve refocused, he heard those unique footsteps coming up the stairs and instantly knew it was EVE'S. They were already indelibly recorded inside his subconscious. He envisioned her movements through the walls, which reminded him of the "Daryl Hannah" character in "Kill Bill 2." Incidentally, before the doorbell rang, her appearance was further validated by the scent of her perfume and the smell of her hair. It was like a mist from the ocean, blended with a spicy whiff of Obsession. The doorbell rang, and he welcomed her and her friend, Samantha. Eve walked with a rhythm in her steps and was dressed in tight blue jeans along with a nice long-sleeved turquoise sweater - accentuating her unique curvaceous figure. Her hair displayed a soft, wet look, accrediting that oceanic odor. Under her arms, she toted over half a dozen fashion magazines, everything from Cosmopolitan to Maxim. He sensed a lengthy interview brewing if time permitted.

MANY SHADES OF HER

Usually, the models brought their clippings. In Eve's case, he had already placed some in a folder for her use. The magazines, now in her hand, looked like they were bookmarked. As he zoomed in, the strips of red tabs became more prominent. Eve flaunted her physique once again. Steve forced those images of her sensuality into the bottom drawer of his mind and got right down to business.

First, he introduced her to Annabelle, who was also a bombshell, except of Latino descent. Regarding looks, Eve's shoes would be a little tight for Annabelle to catwalk. Annabelle smirked on the surface. Steve could tell by the half-smile on Annabelle's face that she felt upstaged. The "chick rivalry" was standard at the office, though masked by many models capable of concealment. Even so, Steve never allowed this contention to get out of hand. His duty was to assess his talent's attitude while keeping it professional — some even tattletales on what was said once they left his office. Annabelle seemed happy with the photos selected for her Zed card. She came over to Steve and hugged him before leaving — something she'd never done before since she signed with the agency two months ago.

Steve, with Anabelle out the door, immediately invited EVE and Samantha over to his desk. Eve sat facing his right and Samantha his left. Steve, still standing, retrieved her folder from the plexiglass folder-holder wall directly behind his desk. Next, he retrieved her application from his desk drawer. Glancing at her documents, he slid down into his rotatable reclining chair. He continued perusing the documents with thoroughness and posture. Steve then asked the question he asked every prospective model in the second interview.

"Tell me a little more about yourself?" Her lips trembled a bit. Then she stuttered, then uttered abruptly.

"Ever since I was a little girl, I spent much time in the mirror. I wanted to take the world by storm and give everyone Eve fever. Additionally, I love fashion and doing fun things, like dancing, hiking, cooking, and sometimes curling up with a book and a nice glass of red wine.

"So, you love to cook? What is your favorite dish?" Steve asked.

Eve responded spontaneously,

"I love making breakfast, any morning dish…I'm all over it. My dinners are in a league by themselves." Samantha attempted to say something but chilled. Steve was glad she did because Eve was on a roll, and he wanted to find out more about casting opportunities for his new model.

"Any interesting life stories?"

MANY SHADES OF HER

This time Samantha butted in.

"It's a miracle she's still alive."

Up to this point in the interview, Samantha hadn't said much. Steve wished she didn't interrupt again, but divine intervention had prompted her to. So, he eagerly welcomed the third-party validation for his potential supermodel. He switched gears and listened intently to Samantha while gazing peripherally at Eve for her reaction.

"What happened?"

He asked.

"Tell me."

Samantha continued:

"Well, she almost died. It was dire."

Samantha's protective instincts were coming alive. Even though, in his opinion, their genes didn't seem to coincide.

Samantha continued:

"She got shot up badly and spent almost a year in the hospital."

Tears were not only welling up in Eve's eyes, but their flow had now created two streams down her beautiful, rosy cheeks, eroding her neatly covered blush.

"Who did? And why? Why would someone do such a thing?"

Steve pried further as his litigating mindset kicked into gear.

"They wanted to kill me,"

Eve said in the voice of a teenager.

Sensing the unfolding of her youthfulness to centerstage, she tried masking her emerging demeanor.

He continued.

"Why? I don't get it,"

Samantha, eager to unload, continued.

"I owned a nightclub in Chicago. One night, she was in attendance. Everyone seemed like they were having a great time. She danced and danced. She mesmerized the audience. Everyone seemed so captivated by her brilliance. It was near closing time when suddenly gunshots rang out. She was shot up multiple times. Consequently, she was hospitalized and placed on life support. It seemed like she'd never recovered. Her recovery was long and difficult. It was tough. Tough for her and tougher for me. I couldn't comprehend what she had to go through. It's a miracle. She's a miracle."

Eve sobbed some more, almost depleting the box of Kleenex as she soaked up the deluge flowing from her eyes and nostrils. Not only was a flood of tears and mucus tricking down, but the torrent of information continued.

MANY SHADES OF HER

Did Steve open up a "can of worms"? The conversation was way too deep. Now, Steve didn't know what to expect. Looking at both women, they seemed mystified.

Samantha sympathetically reached for the last Kleenex in the box to help her hold back her tears. Eve sobbed hysterically as she soaked up the deluge, which was now running down her cheeks.

Steve glanced at the clock on the wall and then back at them. He wanted to hear more about Eve, the epitome of genuine beauty, immersed in reliving her terrible shooting tragedy. But if more tears were shed, there was no professional way to wipe them all away. The Kleenex was sapped. On the other hand, like a great scene, "in-the-moment," Steve Barnes felt like the director who didn't want to say cut!

It was right at this time that Samantha exploded. "Those bastards! Those bastards still have not been caught. They'll pay for this."

Her deluge was now competing with that of Eve's. Samantha, realizing that there was no more available Kleenex, dug into her purse and came up with a folded-up facial tissue. She embarrassedly dried her tears.

"That's messed up."

Steve replied.

"They are still on the loose, huh?"

He asked.

"I closed my business and decided that we'd move to Hollywood. I feel like God sent us to you, which is why you are at the top of our potential list of agencies,"

Samantha remarked, recovering with a smile.

Steve was taken off-guard by the warmth of her curveball grin.

Eve, now with a smile on her face, looked like she'd been revived.

"You are one of a kind, you know how to listen. That's rare."

Eve said.

Complimented, yet flattered, Steve said:

"Thank you."

It now seemed like more than an hour had elapsed since they first sat at his desk. His next appointment was moments away. Was the next model going to be punctual? How would he soothe or describe the dilemma resulting from those four teary eyes?

CHAPTER SEVEN

The doorbell rang, and Steve Barnes buzzed in his next appointment:
"Well, my next appointment is here."
They proceeded to get up from their seats while gathering their personal belongings. There was a knock on the door, it seemed like most people overlooked that buzzer.
"Please wait,"
He said to Eve and Samantha.

They did. He opened the door and asked the entering model to grab water and sit. He grabbed the TV remote and turned on the Television to keep the newly entered Brunette entertained before returning to his desk. This time, he was standing instead of sitting down.

"Do you want to think about it or leave your tear sheets? I could review them and reschedule you for another time."

Eve, now filled with excitement:

"Could we do this in a few days? I so want to get this over."

She continued,

"Elite wants me to come for a second interview next week."

Hearing that statement, Steve realized that he had to get this moving. Mike was already in for her not-too-distant photoshoot.

"How's Sunday at 10:00 AM or 11:00 AM?"

He inquired.

She opened her planner and flipped through its pages. For someone who had gone through so much, she didn't show it physically. Even her hands were beautiful and perfectly manicured, cotton candy pink.

"That's perfect! Let's do 10:00 AM,"

Eve echoed.

Steve schedules her in his planner with ink. Then, he walks them to the door. Samantha hugged him and looked at him in appreciation.

Eve, now recomposed, smiled and left with a firm handshake.

Was Steve closer to getting the yes? Was she going to be a flake? He knew that he was already working deliberately to make it happen. He moved to his next appointment.

CHAPTER EIGHT

Steve Barnes reviewed those numerous tear sheets and developed some wardrobe ideas for Eve's upcoming photo shoot. He also scheduled Mildred, his assistant, was expected to be there for that Sunday, just in case another teary-eyed interlude should emerge. Knowingly, Mildred being there could contribute to a more professional aura to the agency's image. Especially if Eve's protective friend, Samantha, saw it from a third party's POV. After all, Steve didn't want to lose his potential as a supermodel to Ford Models or Elite.

The saying goes: "I have to keep my best foot forward."

Steve was doing just that.

It was 9:30 on Sunday morning. Steve Barnes was sipping his regular early morning cup of coffee and treating this as a regular workday. His morning meditation was already out of the way. He felt relaxed and ready for a big, successful day. The phone rang, and he picked up on the second ring as customary.

"It's a great morning at Ace!"

The voice on the other end responded,

"Mr. Barnes, this is Mildred. I'm afraid I won't make it today; I got called in to be on set. They need me to be featured in a TV commercial, and I was unavailable for the last two weeks."

"No problem; have a great shoot,"

Steven Barnes responded.

He shot several commercials as an actor and was very familiar with those last-minute "rush calls." Plus, that day, he promised himself he would be on top of his game. No negative situation was going to get the best of me. He purposed. Was he ready? In his eyes, he was prepared for this continuing interview with Eve and Samantha, even if he got sprinkled by their emotional deluge this time around. In foresight, he ingeniously picked up a few boxes of Kleenex in case more tears were to be shed. His preparation was paramount. Yes, staying on top of his game was inevitable.

It was 10:00 a.m. The door buzzer sounded. Eve's voice of innocence sounded.

"This is Eve."

"Come on up!"

He said, releasing the intercom on the black phone. He then walked over to the waiting area and tidied up a bit—something Mildred would have done had she shown up as scheduled.

That now all-too-familiar knock was heard. Yes. Eve's knock was different; she possessed lovely, long, slender fingers, making it sound like a genuine romantic wakeup call and strumming on a guitar. He caught himself drifting into those thoughts and reminded himself again: This would be all about business. Nothing else.

He turned on the TV to a Cable News channel and opened the door. Eve, dressed to the nines, looked like a bride ready to meet her bridegroom, except she had no wedding gown, and no man was giving her away. There was no Samantha.

Eve's denim outfit fitted so snugly her curves spoke in loud decibels, and that zipper…just low enough

displayed some upper cleavage. He got a peek of the full contour of her breast but true to her style, it was just a once-over. She entered. He held the door open in anticipation of Samantha's entrance in case she was stuck feeding the meter.
"How was your weekend?"
She inquired.
"Great,"
He said.
Realizing that he was still holding the door open.
"Where's Samantha, feeding the parking meter?"
He questioned.
"She couldn't make it. Weekends are always tough on her. She misses the nightclub back in Chicago. She still goes nuts on the weekends. She so misses not being involved."
Eve responded.
"I like your denim look. I've selected that look from your tear sheets."
Eve followed him to the desk as they proceeded to finalize the choices collectively. They picked out nine very unique looks. Eve looked happy and excited. Steve felt that he had a winner. Happy and excited was a combination of attitudes he looked for in every talent on his roster. It was here.
"When are you available to shoot?"

He asked again.

"I need to check with Samantha to see if she's available to accompany me,"

Eve responded.

Mike was waiting in the wings for Steve to get back to him so he could include Eve in another model's photoshoot.

"Do you want to give Samantha a call? You seem to play well off each other. Plus, she knows your taste."

He reassured Eve.

"I'll catch up with her later, but thanks."

Eve continuing,

"Hey, do you have any pop?"

"Pop?"

He asked.

"Yeah, I could use a Diet Coke or Root Beer."

"Oh, you mean like soda pop?"

He gestured.

She smiled.

"I'll get you one. I never had a pop before."

He reckoned.

"Oh yeah."

Chuckles Eve,

"I forget it's a Mid-West lingo. Still getting acclimated to LA"

She continued.

MANY SHADES OF HER

Steve was oblivious that his back was turned to Eve while reaching the fridge to get her a pop.
She burst out laughing.
He turned to acknowledge her laugh. She was checking him out. Her eyes wandered to other areas of his body. She postured deep in thought. He quickly let the idea of what just transpired leave his head. He brought her the "pop" and popped the lid. She thanked him, and he returned to his desk to peruse her folder and tear sheets.
He noticed her modeling agreement was still unsigned. Was this done purposefully? Did Mildred let this one slip through the cracks? Was she intentionally slacking off? She had been at the office several times after her previous TV commercial gig. Checking these folders was part of her assignment. Those important questions crossed his mind. Additionally, could Mildred have gotten somehow caught up in the chick rivalry?
Steve masked his concerns and got creative. "Everything is set to go except for your signature, " he said as he handed the contract to Eve.
Eve's amber eyes did not even focus on the agreement. Instead with diverted attention, she was looking deeper and deeper into the depths of his soul. Just as she did the first time, our eyes greeted each other, except now with more detail.

Was she questioning my integrity?

Did she locate some bad press about me overnight?

Did she not like my mishandling of Standard American English?

Didn't she not think well of me to make her career?

Steve confidently handed Eve a pen. She took it. She is holding it in the ready-to-sign position, with a smirk now on her face.

"I can't sign this, I wouldn't,"

she said.

"Would you like your lawyer to review it before doing so?"

He encouraged her.

"That's not necessary. Your contract looks legit. I have seen these before. It's just that I have problems signing it. "

He reiterated, in case she was messing with his head, "It's a standard industry contact, Miss Butler. Let me explain. To add you to my roster, we need to have everything in place. That is the standard operating procedure. Maybe you should have Samantha review it with you."

Inside, Steve thought: Why don't you just sign the contract and get this over? You are making me feel like a shrink! That's not my job. Are you trying to make me succumb to bee stings to draw honey? Eve stared at him intently.

MANY SHADES OF HER

He felt as if she read his mind on his last questioning thought.
"I just can't do it. You won't understand."
She said.
Samantha wasn't there, so could she be relying on him for parental guidance?
Steve felt he had enough, so he threw her a curveball.
"What happened, your boyfriend won't let you?
"I don't have one."
She abruptly replied.
This time, Steve looked her up and down.
"You are kidding me. You moved to California from Chicago to pursue a modeling career. Something a lot of women wished they could someday experience. Now you are letting some guy back East tell you - you can't decide for your career."
"No. I don't."
He sized her up and decided to go for the jugular.
"You left him in Chicago and can't deal with the long-distance affair."
"I am not kidding you; I don't have one."
She admitted.
Then, she looked past his eyes into his heart and soul depths. The penetration was so deep that Steve felt like she wanted him. Then she uttered,
"Do you have a girlfriend, Steven?"

CHAPTER NINE

Eve went digging for gold, and he felt like she was about to come away with shovels full of gilt. None of Steve's models had ever called him by his first name.

Should I lie by telling her that I am in a relationship? Steve entertained.

What if she asked to see a picture? He didn't have such a document. Also, if she caught him lying, that contract could remain unsigned.

Steve reflected on her question as it replayed like a scratched-up CD. She was eagerly waiting for his response. He was marinating and massaging his response. Once again, her eyes locked in with his. Now, Steve felt like the table had turned, and he was on center stage, unclothed.

"No,"

He said.

"Why not?"

She asked.

"I've been divorced for a few years now, and I'm focused on Strictly Business right now."

"So, no one at all in your life?"

Eve inquired.

"No."

"Are you…?"

She asks.

"Negative! A relationship could be like a full-time job. Being in love takes work, more than many are ready to undertake."

Even if a relationship with Eve was possible, crossing the line was not in his mindset. Steve has never been involved romantically with any of his models. Mixing business with pleasure always comes back to haunt you, he reckoned. Steve knew she was checking him out. Focus on business, he reminded himself.

"And you are not…?"

"No, I love women. I think they are very special to any man."

His eyes met hers this time and locked into position. He was ready to tell her to go ahead and sign up with Elite Models. But, by this time, he was deep in the beehive with honey and bee stings all over him. Was she ready to sign? Their chess game interlude was interrupted when the phone rang.

Steve answered. It was Mike.

"Mike, let me call you back with a shoot date."

"Why can't you do the photoshoot?"

Eve questioned.

"That's Mike's lane. He is exceptional."

Steve replied.

Eve's eyes were still fixed on him, and she stared as if she wanted to melt the buttons off his close-fitting Hawaiian shirt. As far as Steve was concerned, it was becoming apparent that a working environment wasn't happening for either of them. He still needed confirmation, though, so he resorted to reverse psychology.

Taking it away, he stated,

"So, I guess we can't work together. What are you going to do in Hollywood then? Or are you going to return to Chi-town?"

CHAPTER TEN

Eve went deep into her thoughts and said: "I'll think about it and let you know. Have a good day, Sir. I'll let you know what I think." Even so, Steve felt he was gaining some ground when she addressed him as Sir. Was she ready to sign? Wanting to think about it was said in such a casual way. It sounded very hollow and unintentional.

Were there more stings to endure before I tasted some honey?

After all, she was supposed to be the Franchise. Steve intentionally built up his roster to the point where he was ready for a model of her caliber. If she signs, his agency will have a strong competitive edge against Ford and Elite.

Instead, she got up, stuck her hand out, and shook his. She grabbed her purse, clutched it, and picked up her car keys off his desk. Leaving her magazines, tear sheets, and contracts behind. She was out the door in a hurry.

What have I done? Maybe she was going to be a pain in the ass. At the same time, he sympathized with her past. He entertained that he had a business and couldn't let this bother him that much.

"Well, Elite could have her. Her friend Samantha could open a modeling agency and represent her". Those solutions raced through Steve's head. Annoyed and flustered, he rescheduled his next appointment and meditated for another half an hour to clear his head.

Still, thirty minutes later, he couldn't get Eve out of his head.

MANY SHADES OF HER

CHAPTER ELEVEN

It was another Friday, mid-afternoon. A few weeks elapsed. Eve didn't call back, and neither did Steve Barnes. His agency's roster was expanding without her, anyway. Plus, he thought by now that she had already signed with another modeling agency. Steve's focus was - moving on.

His phone rang at the office. He answered. It was Eve on the other end:

"Thanks for the interview,"

She said politely.

"A happy model is a working model and a working model is a happy model,"

Steve responded.

"Very poetic".

She chuckled.

"Samantha and I would like to invite you over tomorrow after 5:00 PM,"

Eve stated.

"What's going on?"

Steve inquired.

"We thought that dinner would be appropriate. Are you free?"

Eve inquired.

Steve looked at his schedule; it was open. Plus, he saw the possibility that they could be close to making that decision. He was again marinating and massaging the thought: it was in Eve's best interest to ink the contract and join his agency.

"The earliest I can see you would be 6:00 PM,"

Steve replied.

"That's perfect,"

Eve replied.

Steve closed the office at 4:00 p.m. that afternoon. He went home, showered, and headed to their place at

6:00 p.m. He took no paperwork. He was still maintaining his posture. Steve envisioned they would have to return to the office to complete the process if there was still interest.

CHAPTER TWELVE

Steve Barnes researched the location and realized it was a short walk from his office. So, he took the stroll to their address. It was a perfect evening, after all. One of the things he loved about LA over NYC was the fantastic weather, primarily year-round.

Steve had already decided that his visit was going to be all business. He didn't take a pen or the unsigned contract. On the other hand, he knew that visiting two women certainly had its consequences, especially for an accomplished single guy. Plus, Eve was indicating her interest in him. She fitted his mold. Yet, he was not unyielding – maintaining posture. Who knows what they were concocting? This question loomed in his psyche. Even so, he found comfort in alleging Eve would not be alone.

Steve arrived and was buzzed in. The mirrors on the lobby wall of the apartment building displayed much shine and luster. He looked over himself and straightened his crooked shirt collar. Arriving at their apartment, he was treated to an open door. Dressed in gray house slippers and a white sweatsuit, Eve greeted him.

A full-grown, gray-colored cat accompanied Eve. "Meow! Meow!" the cat said. "How polite?" Steve thought. Strangely, though, it seemed too casual except for the cat's presence. Steve felt Eve was not going overboard to impress him. At least not yet.

He was inside, and Eve's beautiful hands closed the door. Before he could take in the ambiance, Eve echoed:

"Samantha's in the kitchen, cooking!"

He maintained his silence.

"How are you?"

She continued. The friendly cat was nibbling at his feet.

"Doing great. You look comfy. What's the cat's name?"

Steve asked.

"Beaver, he's the boss."

"Is he strapped?"

Steve asked jokingly.

"Great sense of humor. Are you?"

Eve responded.

Steve Barnes proceeded to pet Beaver.

Eve wasn't feeling the delay next to the door. So, she expediently led Steve to the kitchen, where Samantha was busily cooking some buffalo wings. His salivary glands went into overdrive. "Good to see you, Steven. What would you like to drink? We have beers, wine, hard liquor, juice, and pop. What's your preference?"

A smorgasbord, he thought. Eve glanced over at him from the reclining chair.

"Some Merlot would be fine."

"Eve, could you get him a Merlot while I finish?"

Samantha said.

Touché, Eve was already on it. She had it as she traversed the room, even in her sweat suit. Steve can imagine Eve as one sexy bartender at Hooters, the Bikini Queen, the lingerie-wearing bride, the centerfold, and so on. She must have read his mind as she profiles and then returns to her curled-up position on the couch across from him.

Steve sat on the couch across from her. Their view was unavoidable. He cheered and then took the first sip.

"Great wine,"

He complimented her.

"Thanks. Someday, I'd like to own a huge wine cellar. How are things at the office?"

Great wine, Great opener, he thought.

He was trying hard to unwind, but he wanted to be precise in his interactions during this visit.

"Things are great. It's a busy week; I added five more models to the roster. Several models auditioned at least once this week. I feel like the agency is ready to make a significant breakthrough. "

He announced.

"How have you been?"

Eve changed the subject briskly and now refocused on him.

"What's going on with Elite?"

Steve inquired.

"Elite? Not happening. I'm considering attending acting school instead."

She confessed.

"Which one?"

He inquired.

"I'm not sure yet. I'm still looking. Maybe Lee Strasberg,"
Eve retorted.
"Great institution, "
he replied.
"Really?"
Eve asked.
"I've studied there in New York."
Said Steve Barnes.
"You did?"
"Yep. I loved the Method Technique. Stanislavski and Strasberg are my heroes…"
Samantha emerged from the kitchen carrying two plates of chicken wings, which she placed on the dining table.
"It's time to eat. Steve, feel free to help yourself."
Eve refilled his glass with wine. Samantha was already seated at the table. Eve put the bottle of wine back in its place and motioned Steve to the table. He followed in tow.
"Let me know what I can do to help, I'll revisit some of my connections. I…"
Samantha interrupted:
"That's so nice of you to do that for her. We are grateful, Mr. Barnes."
Samantha excused herself from the table en route to the kitchen and continued,

MANY SHADES OF HER

"People are all about themselves in this town."

Eve began caressing the less than a half-full glass of merlot with both hands. Hand after hand and stroke after stroke, very meticulously. Steve couldn't help but admire her "French Tip" styled manicure. They complimented her nicely done pedicure, which immediately caught his attention upon his arrival at the door. Steve did not want to focus on her, but she was there in focus like bright daylight, and his eyes were wide open. He couldn't desist.

Samantha rejoined them. She appeared to be not paying attention to Eve's subliminal exchanges. A timer went off in the kitchen. Samantha excused herself from the table and rushed to the kitchen to avoid serving some burnt food. During Samantha's absence, Eve and Steve went mute for at least 90 seconds. In this chess game between them, whoever said the first words wanted this relationship the most.

"How was the wine?"

Eve said in a quiet tone as our eyes locked into his. Steve knew he had already told her that it was great. But he was willing to accommodate once again. Eve's penetrating stare once again entered into his heart and his soul. "Great!"

He could tell she was hungry for more by the look in her eyes.

"It tastes as if the grapes came from a special vine and were kissed daily by the morning dew and then ripened to perfection by the sunrise."

That statement he couldn't withdraw. It was way too late to retreat. Eve had already stepped into his world. Steve felt the tug. After which, the walls crumbled, and the shield to his heart gave way. Defenseless? he was, and she knew it.

"Yes, I'll have another glass of this all-natural, perfectly fermented wine."

Eve poured some gracefully, almost filling up his glass. In haste, he nearly downed the entire glass as if doing so would somehow magically silence the aftershocks and rippling effects marinating inside his heart. Samantha stepped into the frame, returning with some steamy hot biscuits. They smelled so good that she could put Popeyes out of business. Steve stared intently at the platter of biscuits and Samantha and then took Eve in. A woman who could cook and a gorgeous creation in one night. It was so overkill! However, Samantha's obliviousness to her return served as a water hose, pouring water on the fire caused by Eve's heart and mine during her absence. Asked in her customary parental voice:

"Would you like some more wine?"
"Thanks, but I've got to finish some reading tonight, so I'll pass,"
Steve said.
"What type of books do you read?"
Echoed Eve as she gently poured more wine into her glass. Then, he motioned him to have another glass. Steve declined.

Samantha, who had been chewing on our every word since her latest return to the table, was now listening even with more than her ears; her eyes popped.

"Personal development. I've been involved for over 20 years. Love it. It has helped to make me who I am today. Frankly, I don't know where I would be without it."
He remarked.
"Personal development!"
Yelled Samantha.
"So that makes you a bookworm?"
She asked sarcastically. Steve realized that Samantha possessed a split personality. Like a cop, her hot and coldness in a slit second was very noticeable.

"Well, I must say that I read a whole lot. Making or breaking a habit takes 21 days, and I see this as a great habit. One is worthwhile for anyone who

wants to progress in life. So, I boarded the train…"
Steve Barnes articulated.
"Interesting,"
Said Eve. At the same time, taking another sip from the almost empty glass.
"I'm fascinated…"

Eve continued.
"A consistent reader, huh?"
Interrupted Samantha.
Steve placed a biscuit and some chicken on his plate and dug in to balance the multiple glasses of wine.
"Wow! Hot and juicy! "
he exclaimed.
Eve looked across at Samantha, and they exchanged smiles. Samantha placed some of that delicious food onto Eve's plate and then loaded up her plate. Cooks typically have a small appetite after being exposed to all that food odor during cooking. But not so with Samantha. She inhaled all that food and was now packing it away.
Meanwhile, Eve's lips dropped like honey…as he devoured the succulent chicken wings. Steve got carried away in thinking again and wished to lick her greasy fingers, but he immediately abandoned that thought. Pulling his foot out of his mouth on this

one wasn't easy, as the food in his stomach was not speedily catching up with all the wine he consumed. He saw Eve as a consumer, so it was no wonder she envisioned owning a cellar. Steve drank only occasionally. His preference is a cold beer that can be passed out shortly thereafter. However, if a woman offers wine and she's curled up enjoying hers, what type of man would say,
"Let me have a beer," when she's searching for compatibility in her domain?
"Reading is good!"
Uttered Samantha. She seemed to have digested her food and thought about his hobby.
"You can say that. It keeps me focused. Well, talking about focus, I need to get going, but I've enjoyed it. Samantha, thanks for the invitation, the great meal, and, most of all, your kind hospitality. Thanks for interviewing with the agency and extending this dinner invite. As mentioned, let me know if I could assist with your chosen endeavors."
"Thanks for coming,"
Eve replied.
She walked him to the door.
"I will let you know what happens with this whole acting deal."
Steve sensed some degree of letdown in her voice. Did she mention attending acting school to get out

of signing with the agency? He asked underneath his breath.

The cat moseyed past him, once again trying to upstage Eve. This time, it was continuously licking its right paw.

"She was right. He was the boss – he saw me in and out."

Steve said quietly to himself.

Peripherally, though, he gleaned an extended look at her ocean-scented hair as she sneaked into his arms with a long-tight embrace. She whispered,

"Steven, I'll see you soon."

Her breath and BO smelled of spicy chicken wings, sweet wine, Obsession Perfume, and raw honey. That scent stayed with him for the rest of the night.

CHAPTER THIRTEEN

It was now Monday evening—four weeks since Eve's first interview at Steve Barnes' office. Steve was busy getting the office ready for the next business day. Thoughts of Eve were still occupying space in his mind. That hair scent and…?

The ringing of the phone interrupted the flow. He picked up. Eve's voice was on the other end as if she knew he had her indelibly on his mind.

"Thanks for coming over on Saturday evening, Steven. We enjoyed your company."
"So glad you did. How's Beaver?"
He said curtly.
"Cuddly as always. He has a habit of nibbling at people's feet. Hope he didn't scare you."
Eve said apologetically.
"No worries, I love cats; they are so in the moment when they do what they do. He's so hospitable. Most actors find cats such a pleasure to watch, especially when one is honing the craft."
"I'd never really thought of that. You are such a wealth of knowledge and a wise man. By the way, Samantha and I want a change of pace, get out and enjoy LA more. We would love to come out if you hear of any events."
Steve already knew what was happening on the upcoming Friday night. His friend Michael, who also owned a modeling agency, had invited him to his birthday party on a late-night boat cruise in the Los Angeles Harbor. Michael told Steve he could bring some ladies. Steve, admittedly, anxiously thought about inviting Eve several times but changed his mind every time the thought re-occurred. He did so again before she called, mainly for fear of fueling the fire in this brewing relationship. Her timing was immaculate. Women

are such intuitive individuals; he internalized as his thoughts wandered.

"There's a boat ride coming up this Friday. My agent friend Michael, from another modeling agency, is celebrating his birthday. Both of you are invited to attend as my guests. The boat sails from Marina Del Rey at 7:00 p.m. Let me know if you and Samantha would like to attend.

"For sure, count us in. Awesome. You live nearby. We can even get you."

She retorted.

Mildred was using his Mazda to run her errands, so Eve's kind gesture was greatly appreciated.

"See you Friday at 6:00 p.m. Please call me if there are any changes."

He suggested.

Steve Barnes saw this as an opportunity to connect Eve in Hollywood, possibly with some actors mentored by great acting coaches. Steve extended the courtesy by inviting his two roommates – Tom and his new weekend's house crasher, Maxwell.

CHAPTER FOURTEEN

It was now Friday, and after a busy day at the office, Steve rushed home and readied himself for the party. Eve called, stating she was running about 15 minutes behind. Steve, in afterthought: why didn't he tell her 6:45? After all, he grew up with five sisters and, very early in life, understood women needed extra time to get ready.

MANY SHADES OF HER

Plus, Eve mentioned during her interview that while growing up, she spent a lot of time looking at herself in the mirror – he chuckled to himself, primping. He closed the door and sauntered toward the lobby. She was running late—fear of missing the boat, in Steve's POV, sunken in. Boats leave on time unless we are willing to swim to them.

Moments later, a white Jaguar pulls up outside, preceded by some awesome reggae music as the driver's window rolls down. Steve cut his teeth on that kind of music from the Caribbean and began swaying mentally.

Eve stepped out. She was solo and looked hot. Steve thought about Samantha possibly meeting them there. Going back to get her at the apartment would dilute our schedule, and the boat would depart without us. The latter was closest.

Upon entering the car, Eve informed him Samantha wouldn't make it. Eve said Samantha's patient needed her. He'd learned that Samantha worked as a caretaker for an elderly woman. Eve backed up her alibi, stating that she would call and cancel attending, but Samantha told her that she should go because she could do lots of networking.

"That's right. You never know who you'll meet," Steve responded assumingly.

MANY SHADES OF HER

Steve felt reassured that multiple other top industry people would be in attendance. That's just how his friend, Mike, rolled.

Eve was stoked. She lowered the music a little and reached inside her purse. Retrieving a flask, she unscrewed the cover, unveiling contents resembling Whisky. It was.
"I brought us some Whisky, "
she said.
"Interesting. Makes for a great night."
He said.
"You may have the honors of…"
Eve said while passing the flask his way.
"Thanks. It's just not me. Red wine or beer is always preferred."
Steve said.
He was not about to partake now or later. Hard liquor was no longer his style. He detested hangovers. She returned it to her purse and brought out an Altoids container With four neatly rolled joints. The aroma of chronic weed gave Steve instant contact. His first thought after that unintentional unlit whiff was: those smell awesome. Steve knew he would need one later to maintain balance while the boat sailed. It was an understatement that Eve came

MANY SHADES OF HER

out to party that night. They shared one joint and arrived at the dock in super high spirits.

MANY SHADES OF HER

CHAPTER FIFTEEN

The moon was full, and Eve giggled so much it should have been outlawed. It was a clear indication that she was already high. Steve discovered the high side of her was filled with nothing but fun, laughter, and soulfulness. That chronic weed certainly worked its magic on Eve. She was happy as a kid in a candy store and ready to…

MANY SHADES OF HER

They toured the three-decked ship, which was already music-filled. Every deck featured a DJ playing a different genre of music.

After the boat's anchor was lifted, they ran into Steve Barnes' roommates, Tom and Maxwell. Both African Americans, Tom was the kind of guy who portrayed himself as a Casanova. He always had to be with a woman. He was always entertaining nightcaps at the crib. While Maxwell, on the other hand, was a little bit more selective in his limited choice of women; he was nursing the painful hurts of a fresh divorce. Regardless of their stance, they both gave Steve those jealous, amazed Manship looks as if to say:

"What the heck did you do to land her."

Eve was hotter than July. However, they had no idea that it was the other way around. They taunted, and Steve's chest grew mass. The bottle of Guinness in Steve's hand was almost empty, and the screwdriver in Eve's glass needed replenishment.

Steve picked up another round of drinks at the bar and put a Heineken in his two roommates' hands. The tour continued, and they later ran into Michael on the lower deck. Though he was not alone, he had an entire wing, as several women were in his company. What a way to spend one's birthday. Steve pondered and immediately introduced Michael to his guests. Like the magnet she was, Eve bonded quickly with the women in Mike's clique.

Christina, a Steve Barnes acting class student, was also present. She knew Michael, who also frequented our acting school. Christina worked as if she were a female "Larry King." After hearing how Steve fit into the scheme of things with Eve, she openly declared that she didn't see any chemistry between Eve and Steve.

Christina was petite and frequented by men of celebrity status. Steve understood how much misery loved the company, so he chose not to let her comment spoil the night for Eve and himself.

CHAPTER SIXTEEN

Steve Barnes and Eve continued networking while they partied. The moon was ripe, and its reflection on the water was a testament to its illumination. Eve's shadow was emerging as she became more and more lit. It was like the moon came out, and her shadow emerged. The drinks and the two joints went in, and her shadow materialized. On the second upper deck of the ship, Eve's eyes captured a pole while the music crescendo. Eve gravitated, and from it, she swung. Her wild side was evolving, and strangely, Steve liked it. She immediately drew a captive audience. Eve was clothed, but his imagination was running wild. Steve was trying to keep his cool, but what she brought to the table visually and sublimely deprived him of that right.

It became increasingly apparent to him that Eve was sweet and innocent, like an angel when sober, but shades of her placed her as a devil in disguise when under the influence. As Eve continued dancing, the applause of a growing crowd escalated. Spectators were throwing dollar bills on the floor in front of her. Deep inside, Steve was praying she didn't disrobe. That would be publicly embarrassing him on this first date.

A woman standing across from Steve and drinking a screwdriver couldn't keep her eyes off him. There was a mutual feeling among the men on the ship – they wanted Eve. She picked up on that intruder of her space, and consequently, that costly stare resulted in a verbal confrontation between them. The crowd, cheering for Eve a minute ago, was poised to break up a simmering duel.

The quarrel intensified.

MANY SHADES OF HER

What did he cause? It was visible on Steve's face. Would someone have to fish both women out of the deep Los Angeles waters?
Steve prayed:
"Dear God, please don't let this get out of hand." Swimming had never really been Steve's strong suit. If this brewing fight escalates and goes overboard, he'll have to take a crash course on some swimming techniques or strap on a life jacket.
By now, Eve and that obstructive patron were close in each other's faces. When Eve removed her high heels, Steve sensed it would get ugly sooner rather than later. That other party retreated, and so did Eve. Steve relaxed somewhat when Eve cooled her heels and returned to the pole. He breathed a sigh of relief. By this time, her newly converted fans were cheering wildly. Eve was their warrior princess. She danced and danced and danced some more. The DJ caught on and played some of his best pole-dancing style tracks. Men were now throwing dollar bills at Eve's feet. Steve was somewhat disturbed by her uninhibited behavior, but on the other hand, she looked so hot in the interim that she turned him on.
Eve instantly became the star of her one-woman show, improvised and uncensored. People she'd never met and others who didn't even know her name were cheering for her, except without pom-

poms. Some smiled and winked at her as she passed by. Others gravitated to her like a magnet.

The ship dropped its anchor, and Steve delightfully carried her ashore. Steve's roommates, Tom and Maxwell, couldn't understand what they had and were currently witnessing.

Steve has lived with his roommate, Tom, for almost a year. Maxwell is a newbie who frequents on weekends. They have never had the opportunity to witness that side of Steve. His game is on. They even openly wish he'd drop Eve on the parking lot's pavement.

To not embarrass himself and spoil the night, Steve carried her safely down the steps and off the ship, like he was born doing. Eve hugged his neck with both arms and basked in the method of transportation after such an eventful night. Once again, she drew additional fans and spectators.

CHAPTER SEVENTEEN

They arrived at the parking lot after touring it in search of her car. She became a one-shoe Eve. This is a Cinderella-like episode: After losing her slipper, he thinks of and helps her retrieve it. In this scene, Steve has heard and read the story of the princes more times than he can count. Now, in a real-life situation, he can act it out. Steve recovers his tracks. He finally comes up with the missing shoe.

Eve caught on, and they shared a wet kiss. She sobered up by the time they found her Jaguar. That episodic fairy tale was now a cherished performance letdown. Was she okay to drive? Steve trusted her ability to take the wheel, and she delivered.

They arrived at his apartment door. Eve was carrying her shoes along with her purse in her hands.

Barefooted, with her hand locked inside, Steve Barnes entered.

Surprisingly, Maxwell and Tom were still up and watching TV. Something was beyond the norm for both of them after 2:00 a.m. on a Saturday. Steve said:

"Hi,"

as they passed them like an exam and went into his bedroom.

Eve and Steve were now in instantaneous full embrace. Their syncing loomed much more than in the movie Mr. and Mrs. Smith. They passionately began to share each other's passion. Pent up inside for each other since they first met.

Steve found and played some soft music to compliment.

In addition to discovering much about each other in that little room. Eve proved herself to be a tigress in bed. Steve realized Eve was as passionate about him as he was about her. Sensing that it was time to leave and get her home, a shower helped to revitalize both. They exited the bathroom to the sun's early morning rays peeping through the window.

Eve checked her cell phone, which seemed filled with unanswered calls. She had muted it before getting on the ship.

"Are you Ok?"

Steve asked with concern. She smiled and hugged him tightly.

"I've got to go."

She whispered sensually in Steve's ear. Steve held her hand and walked her out of the apartment to her car. Eve's embrace of Steve's tall frame indicated their mutual desire, more so than when they first met. He opened the car door for her and sealed their extended, eventful first date with a wet, steamy early morning kiss.

CHAPTER EIGHTEEN

It was Monday. It was now back to work as usual. Plans were in the works for a major fashion show at the Hollywood Highlands in Hollywood. While Steve was planning this significant event, he couldn't escape thinking about Eve and their woven relationship.

MANY SHADES OF HER

He encapsulated the relationship thus far and concluded they were rushing into it. Yet, he wanted her in his life. She left a yearning effect on him, and she could have been the boss. A void was opening in Steve's life when she wasn't around. Unbelievable but real, could it be he was falling for this woman?

Steve had been divorced for multiple years, and Eve was the second woman to enter his life since. Eve was exceptionally comfortable in bed, and he relished her sensuality.

Subsequently, she had been in a fight and was beginning to rock Steve's world.

Knowing that he'd encountered two failed relationships, all within the past two years, creating further damage to his heart, he had previously dodged like a bullet, on the other hand, Eve had not been involved with any man for over three years. Steve was oblivious to this as she had never disclosed the tenure of her relationship. She said she didn't have a boyfriend; they had already created this brush fire in the affair. It felt like no water would be able to put it out. Two doors were closed, and this new window of sensuality was opened and branded - Eve.

While Steve was busy organizing the upcoming fashion show, he called and asked if she would be his date. It was on a Friday night, which magically worked well in her calendar. Friday night came as if it was the next day.

Steve sent a limo to get Eve and bring her to the venue, but first, making a pitstop at Steve's crib. Steve was great at delegating, plus the facility wrapped their previous event at least half an hour later. They enjoyed a few glasses of wine and some foreplay. It was almost showtime, so they headed to the Hollywood Highlands.

Even though the event was delegated to capable hands, and Steve's phone call let them know he was running behind, everyone was still waiting for Steve to proceed. Some of the women he put in charge gave him the evil eye as he rolled in with Eve. Once again, her centerstage attitude gave them a whiff of black pepper. Their ineptness didn't sit well with Steve. Their posts were assigned even before he dropped Eve the invite. Plus, he was the boss and cut their checks.

Steve made the necessary phone calls, including the most important one to Robert, the club's promoter. During that conversation, he learned that they had scheduled another event for that evening, which cut into the time of his fashion show. The Highlands was not only a premier event space but a mega one. This action on Robert's part was unorthodox and was setting up the show to end prematurely. That wasn't fair to the fans, the talent, or Steve. Plus, it wasn't in the contract. So, Steve had it out over the phone with him. Steve visually expressed his displeasure with the dropping of the ball. To say the least, Steve was pissed.

"I'll be there soon, Mr. Barnes,"

Robert promised.

Steve got off the phone and returned to the running of the show.

CHAPTER NINETEEN

Things got worse at this Hollywood Highlands event. Some Models were unhappy. Steve Barnes knew this, but at this point, it became more apparent as dozens of eyes were focused on him. It wasn't his fault the facility screwed up, but the buck stopped with him in their opinion. Some gave him looks like he was blindly caught in a vice with the wrong woman.

MANY SHADES OF HER

Eve could not cool it, with raised eyebrows and a smirk on her face. Her additional body language said:

"Yeah, that's my guy!"

Her authority was pissing people off, mainly Steve's staff. He had much under control, but Eve tactfully inserted herself on defense. Most of them saw it as if she was taking ownership of him. But deep inside, he was kindhearted, and most of his camp took advantage of this sweetness. On the other hand, Eve had just witnessed – the man of steel side of Steve, and she loved it.

Through all of this debacle, Eve kept cheering Steve on.

"Get him. Don't take their crap!"

She echoed, borderline Gangsterism. If their looks were a machine gun, Steve would have been executed at that point.

After his pep talk, Steve met with the models waiting to take the stage and complimented them on the great job they were doing. Esther remarked that she was having such a great time that she couldn't wait to grace the stage. It was her first time on the all-important catwalk.

Robert Alston, the venue's director, showed up breathlessly and apologized for the catastrophe that was caused. He offered to give drinks on the house to Steve's entire team, which he did. Robert also asked Steve if he could come to a compromise by finishing by 9:45 p.m., which equated to 45 minutes later than scheduled. Steve agreed.

MANY SHADES OF HER

CHAPTER TWENTY

Eve had stepped into Steve's world, causing a colossal transformation. Not only did she upstage *Devil in a Blue Dress*, but on that Friday night, she was dressed in black, and her recent emergence brought on and rattled like California earthquakes in his world — for him among women and Eve among men. Eve's outfit embodied her creativity; she displayed lingerie lines and bathing suits during the fashion show. Guys were whistling and hollering as she cat-walked.

Not only was she hot and beautiful, but the news quickly spread that she was seeing Steve. To most, Steve was all business. However, most were treated to a premiere of him with his Mack on.

It was time for Steve's closing remarks as they called Steve on stage.

"Ladies and gentlemen, this has been an incredible night. Thanks to you – our fans. I realize most of our audience are sports lovers. I love sports. Not only are sports exciting to watch. Sports always bring out the combativeness of athletes. Michael Jordan, one of the greatest players to ever play the game of basketball, displayed a tremendous belief in himself. In 1990, while playing for the Chicago Bulls, his inspiration helped him score three times his jersey number by dropping 69 points against the Cleveland Cavaliers. To succeed at anything, you must first believe that you can. Wishing will never put you in the driver's seat. Most often your belief can be stretched out like the waiting process involved in the growth of a Chinese Bamboo Tree. Understanding the growth process of this unique tree will certainly dispel those doubts and fears you hold about yourself - those imaginary walls deterring you from ever becoming who you were always meant to be. In my opinion, this is a classic example of doubt and faith being put to the test.

You take a tiny seed, plant it, water it, and fertilize it for a whole year, and nothing happens. The second year, you water and fertilize it, and nothing happens.

In the third year, you water and fertilize it; nothing has come up yet.

In the fourth year, you water and fertilize it, but still nothing. In the fifth year, you continue to water and fertilize the seed. Sometime during the fifth year, the Chinese bamboo tree sprouts and grows NINETY FEET IN SIX WEEKS.

Thanks to the Hollywood Highlands, our models, and the entire team. We'll see you at our next event."

Cheers came from the crowd as if Steve had beaten the clock, burying a three-pointer behind the arc.

Eve's was the loudest. Making her way backstage, she embraced Steve Barnes and planted a kiss on him.

"That was so great. What a monologue. What a speech."

Eve said.

The show was a wrap.

The meet and greet began.

Eve stood by Steve's side, and she belonged. They looked so fashionable together. Photo-ops spiked.

Steve liked it that way. Coming from the school, a man is noticed by the woman beside him. Eve brought him massive attention. More and more people were coming up to congratulate Steve on hosting such an awesome event. This was great, but Eve and Steve would rather be someplace else, wrapped up in each other.

Steve looked across at Eve, and the look in her eyes indicated that the feeling was reciprocal. So, they proceeded to leave. Christina, who'd assisted in coordinating the event, saw them heading towards the exit. She had volunteered to help Steve with the event. During the finale, she was trying desperately to get Eve's attention. Christina wanted so badly to butter up. It was now like a burning obsession, so much so that she dashed in their direction.

"You guys looked so good together tonight."

She said.

Eve and Steve responded with "thank you" simultaneously. Steve looked at her, smiled, and winked at Eve.

"What's your name?"

Eve asked.

"Christina!"

She replied enthusiastically.

Maxwell, one of the participating models, came over and shook Steve's hand. Christina took this

MANY SHADES OF HER

opportunity to get Eve's 411. They exchanged phone numbers. It seemed like Christina had finally made her dream come true. Eve and Steve catch a cab and head back to Steve's place.

CHAPTER TWENTY-ONE

The night was still young even though the fashion show had wrapped. Steve needed to unwind. Additionally, Eve sensed he was starving and volunteered to fix him her special meal - breakfast. She knew the way to a man's heart was his stomach, and Steve, a Caribbean man, was multiplied by two. She felt his heart was in her hands and was well worth two in the bushes, so her

MANY SHADES OF HER

objective was to keep him. Steve spent so much time at the office – his refrigerator was bare.

"Let's go to the supermarket and buy some groceries, Steve,"
She suggested, although it was early Saturday morning.
They returned to his crib in less than an hour.
"I'm going to make you some great breakfast,"
Eve said as they entered the door.
Surprisingly, Maxwell made it back to the crib while they were gone. He was on the couch watching TV. At the same time, Steve went to the kitchen and unpacked the groceries.
"I'm going to my car to get my headshots."
Maxwell said while going through the door. Not long before, Eve joined Steve, dressed down in her undies. Eve profiled and cat walked as she entered the kitchen. He was all for it if this was how she wanted to make him breakfast. Steve had no choice but to follow suit.
Prior, Steve very seldom made breakfast. Some may classify him as a workaholic. Very rarely was he able to enjoy a great meal. Whenever he had a good meal, it was from the Thai Restaurant across the street from his job. Most times, it was rushed. Now, suddenly, his kitchen was not only buzzing with

MANY SHADES OF HER

activity, filled with a mixed aroma, but it was also hot and sensually captivating. Steve cracked and beat the eggs while Eve stirred the grits in the saucepan. Then Steve inserted the sliced bacon into the scrambled eggs being cooked. Eve fetched the ice and placed it in a pitcher while Steve poured the juice therein. Steve fetched the eating utensils while she served the meal onto the two large plates. Eve held the candle, and Steve lit it for her.

CHAPTER TWENTY-TWO

Eve retrieved the dishes and served the meal. They sat down to eat at the table while staring into each other's eyes. Eve looked so great; the food became secondary as foreplay took priority. From Tom's room, his Television blasted. Even though Tom was considered a lady's man, none had come through these doors in the likeness of Eve.

Steve was tickled as the night progressed. Eve fed him some pancakes with a smile. He gently returned the favor. To Steve, there was always a fascination about checking out a woman's mouth. Eve had terrific teeth. She reminded Steve that his acting coach stressed having great teeth in Hollywood.
They heard a key turn in the front door. By the sound of the footsteps, Steve knew it was Maxwell's. He entered.
"Something smells great in this kitchen."
He said.
His eyes magnified as he entered, staring at them at the table.
"Would you like me to fix you a plate?"
Eve asked.
"Sure, I love grits!"
He replied.
She did fix him a plate.
"This is special, some grits."
Steve said as he passed him en route to put on some music.
Steve Barnes was unsure if Maxwell was more involved in putting his headshots in envelopes or eavesdropping on their episode.
After partaking in that healthy breakfast, Eve and Steve did the dishes together. He washed while she rinsed. They tidied up the kitchen and passed

MANY SHADES OF HER

Maxwell, half asleep on the couch, on their way towards the bedroom. Maxwell's plate sat on his lap – swept clean. Sensing too much indulgence, he awoke and went through the door abruptly.

Steve and Eve looked at each other and led Eve into the bedroom.

MANY SHADES OF HER

CHAPTER TWENTY-THREE

As the morning dragged toward sunrise. Foremost on Steve's mind was to spend quality time with his new find – Eve. He cranked up the music. Revisiting his tenure as a DJ back in New York. Eve liked the tracks, which swiftly put her in her creative element. It was apparent from the start that they couldn't get enough of each other. Nothing else seemed to matter, except they had no wedding vows.

Steve realized Eve was so much more than a woman; she was an amazing, wonderful experience. Void of many such recent experiences, this one mattered from Steve's POV. Having her for keeps crossed his mind several times as they lay in bed, interweaving in each other's embrace.

Ironically, Eve's cell phone rang. How Steve hoped she wouldn't answer it. His wish was granted when it stopped ringing after the seventh or eighth ring. He assumed it wasn't essential or could have been an incorrect dialed number. About 5 minutes elapsed, and the apparent persistent caller was back at it. Again, Eve didn't answer. Steve cuddled her some more. His investigative skills kicked in. It dawned on him that whoever was trying to reach Eve was also trying to get him.

Then he released his hold from around her and reached for the phone.

"Hello"

He answered in a somewhat distracted voice.

"Steven, is Eve there?"

The person asked in a rather upsetting, lonely voice. He was familiar with Samantha's voice, but she had relinquished that possessive voice for a rather lonely, possessive one.

"She is. She is here with me. Is everything Ok?"
Steve inquired.

"No. It's not."
Samantha responded in increased decibels.
"That's my WIFE, Steven!"
Samantha continued.
"Really? I'm so…"
"Steven, please let her know I am waiting for her.'
"I will get back,"
Steve hung up the phone.
He looked over at Eve, sitting straight up in the bed. He eased up next to her, gently caressing her body.
"Eve, your husband wants you."
Steve relayed.
"Why did he have to ruin my night?"
Eve asked.
"I don't know, but I wish you had told me this was happening. I would not have gotten in this deep …I don't believe in wrecking or breaking up your marriage."
Steve said.
"We've been married for several years, Steven."
He stared at her while weighing the matter.
"I've got to go,"

MANY SHADES OF HER

Eve said.

On the other hand, Steve wanted her to stay. Even so, she was bent on leaving.

"Would you like me to call you a cab?"

Steve asked with concern.

"I'll find my way home."

She responded with tears in her eyes and proceeded to get dressed. After being fully attired, they embraced, not wanting to let each other go. Eventually, Eve grabbed her purse and left the room as Steve walked her out.

Maxwell returned and was up and watching TV in the living room. That empty plate was now on the center table. I don't know if Maxwell had heard what went down, but he echoed.

"You are leaving? I'll give you a ride home."

Steve saw them both go through the apartment door, and he handed Eve her forgotten hooped earrings.

Steve admitted he was saddened to see her leave. The next day, Maxwell told him that he had given her a ride home and that she looked petrified.

CHAPTER TWENTY-FOUR

After that long, unforgettable night, the thought of them getting back together again waned.

Eve was wrapped up in a love triangle that could be disastrous for all parties involved. Although loving memories of her still intermittently messed up with

Steve's emotions, living just a few blocks from each other proved too close for comfort. Plus, breaking away from a possessive Samantha seemed problematic for Eve. On the other hand, losing Eve was not an easy pill for Steve to swallow.

Christina, who had bonded with Eve at the fashion show, was still attending his acting class. Steve noticed she now had a chip on her shoulder. There was no doubt in his mind Christina knew about the breakup between Eve and himself. Women always seem to know what's going on in the love lives of their peers. No wonder twelve of them can go to the restroom together and although they were strangers could emerge as buddies.

Christina was the kind of woman who buddied up to just about everybody. She knew what was going on in just about everybody's backyard. Christina talked about every African American male celebrity she'd ever wanted to sleep with.

About a year later, one day, Steve overheard Christina talking to another actress at school. Eve was the topic of their conversation. Christina claimed they were communicating and that Eve was looking for a place to live. Was she saying this because Steve was present or because she just wanted to gossip about Eve? Steve had moved on and went into the limousine business as a chauffeur.

Christina and Steve were assigned a scene, to put up in acting class. Their coach felt that her feistiness was great for the dramatic piece. During the rehearsal, Christina asked Steve.

"You talked to your girl lately?"
"It's been a while,"
He responded.
"Homegirl moved in with me last week."
Steve had called Eve on multiple occasions to no avail.

MANY SHADES OF HER

CHAPTER TWENTY-FIVE

Christina had a teenage daughter whom she brought to class on some occasions, and every grown-up person's conversation was embellished. Steve didn't want to be on the in, but he had gone to Christina's apartment on a few occasions prior, to pick up a nickel bag. Her apartment was a tiny one-bedroom. He imagined another adult sharing that space was hard to comprehend. But when breakups occur, people put their pride aside and settle. Steve thought Eve was dealing with a second breakup within those two months. She could have said bye to Samantha or vice versa. Eventually, Steve moved on and was already restructuring his life. The modeling agency was now a thing of the past as he began writing.

Maxwell, his roommate, even collaborated with him on their first treatment. One Sunday, he invited Steve to church, and Steve loved it so much that he began improving his life.

Something was changing deep down inside of him. One Sunday morning, the pastor spoke on sex and the benefits of living a pure life. These blessings included God's favor and a life of honoring God with your body, which is classified as his Temple.

Steve grew up listening to that philosophy and mindset in church and yearned for such again. He wanted his life to be the one his mother envisioned when she dragged him to church every week. Plus, he needed to know that his involvement with another woman in the future was for real, and most importantly, she didn't belong to someone else, creating a triangular debacle.

He closed the agency mainly because things got tight financially. Models were turning down auditions. Lethargy on their part was paramount. So much that it was beginning to hurt his survival. To avoid going bankrupt Steve had no choice but to close the doors while exploring other options. He started to write his first screenplay. Steve saw much potential down the road. Driving limousines was part of his resume when he lived in New York City. It paid great money at the time. So much that it helped him pay his expenses by relocating to Los Angeles. Steve decided to reengage with that occupation here in California while pursuing a writing and acting career.

CHAPTER TWENTY-SIX

Through word of mouth, Christina soon learned Steve chauffeured as a limo driver. She called one evening, wanting to know what the rates were. However, she didn't lock in a reservation. It wasn't long before he received a call from Eve. Steve knew it was her, as her number appeared on his caller ID.

"Steven, this is Eve. How are you?"

She said in that sometimes innocent voice.

"Doing just great. Sitting here at the LAX waiting to pick up a client whose flight was delayed. How are things with you?"

He inquired.

"Things are different. I've moved and now live in Culver City. It's a change. Anyway, my birthday is coming up…"

She said.

"I know!"

He interrupted.

"I wanted to know if you could drive me that night for about 4 hours. It's going to be me along with two or three other friends."

Eve stated.

"Do you have your schedule intact?"

Steve asked.

"I do,"

Replied Eve.

"What time do you need to be picked up, and from where?"

"At 9:00 p.m. Would it be ok to email you the pickup and drop off locations?"

MANY SHADES OF HER

'That would be great. Please call me a week before to confirm."

His client was coming down the stairs from the arrival terminal with his two carry-ons.

"I will"

Eve said, ending the call.

To Steve, it would be like driving two other clients, not knowing the identities of those in her party. However, something inside him yearned to see if and how much she was evolving into a better person. Not that he had plans of getting back together with her, but the change in him was taking him to new heights. He recently dropped his first book. Which was on bookshelves. The good news is that following absenteeism is always like a breath of fresh air to the inquirer. In this case, his curiosity was getting the best of him. On the other hand, if not, she could have picked hundreds of drivers for her event. She sent that email and called to reconfirm a week ahead. It was a busy Friday the day prior, and Steve scheduled accordingly so he would not have to send another driver on that job. It was customary to schedule whenever a driver got overbooked on any particular day.

CHAPTER TWENTY-SEVEN

Steve Barnes readied himself and headed out to Eve's place. He didn't know what to expect. But he assumed that it was going to be all business. His romantic feelings for Eve had subsided. However, curiosity is known to have killed the cat.

He pressed the buzzer. She invited him up and then buzzed him in. They greeted each other with a hug.

He noticed that there was a difference in her instantly. She had lost the glow she'd possessed when they were together. Eve was not the happy person she used to be. Steve realized that she was home alone. Eve informed him her boyfriend had gone to the store to get some beer and that he'd be right back.

"Have a seat!"

She said after our embrace.

"I am so glad to see you. You look great. Have you been working out?"

She continued.

Not wanting this to be Déjà vu. So, Steve calculated his every move while measuring hers with a yardstick.

"Can I get you something to drink? Wine? Beer? Water? Whatever you want."

She asked.

"Water is fine."

Steve responded.

"No wine? Don't drink anymore? You always liked Merlot. Come on it is my birthday."

Eve encouraged him in that sweet, innocent voice. It's a habit for Steve not to drink alcohol before or while driving a client.

"But thanks, I'm so happy it's your big day, and you chose to celebrate it,"

MANY SHADES OF HER

Steve said.

She had already brought Steve a glass of water, so he initiated the cheers. The door opened, and a guy walked in with two shopping bags under his arms. Steve noticed the six-packs and the silhouettes of the bottles he was carrying in those shopping bags.
She jumped up from her seat and helped him with one of the bags.
"Jeff, this is Steve Barnes, our driver. He's the gentleman I told you about. He owned a modeling agency in Hollywood."
"Thanks for showing up to drive us tonight. What are you drinking, soda?"
 Jeff inquired.
Eve assured Jeff,
"He'll have a drink with us later. "
" Are we ready?"
Jeff asked Eve.
"Steven, I didn't pick up ice, so could we stop at a 7/11 on our way? If we need more liquor, I could get some also."
Steve continued.
"I have ice and champagne, so I think we're good..."
Steve responded.

MANY SHADES OF HER

They poured themselves two drinks. While Steve grabbed one of the shopping bags and led the way downstairs and out to the limousine.

CHAPTER TWENTY-EIGHT

They were mobile and Jeff lit up a marijuana joint and shared it with Eve. Jeff handed it to Steve, inviting him to get a share. Once again Steve declined. He was semi-high, anyway, unintentionally, by the contact he'd received as a result of their second-hand smoke.

Eve instructed Steve to pick up another couple on his way. A few minutes later, he opened the door for those guests to join them.

MANY SHADES OF HER

Eve wanted to enjoy the glitz and glamour of Hollywood at night, so very soon, they were entrenched in the stop-and-go traffic of the scenic LA nightlife.

Jeff seemed like he was the quiet type. At least this was evident by Eve doing the bulk of the talking. That was her strong suit. Her guests laughed constantly at her whacky jokes. They no doubt realized that she was as high as a kite.

They were concluding the tour of Hollywood as Eve made phone calls to find a suitable club.

"Where is the right club for us?" She repeated this phrase at least six times. After several phone calls, Eve found a club she was happy with and informed Steve to make that his next stop.

It wasn't long before the black stretch limo pulled up outside. They insisted that Steve join them. So, after their exit, Steve found a parking spot, got out, and proceeded inside the club in tow. It was less than two minutes after entering this ghetto nightspot, evident by its funky outside decor. It wasn't Steve's style. Inside the club was wall to wall.

The night evolved, and the event grew in size. Suddenly, Steve noticed several people huddled with drawn semi-automatics, and they were all pointing at Eve. Several women were now joining

the attackers. Eve was in the spotlight seemingly about to get shot.
What did she do?
Did she say something obnoxious to someone?
Did she look at someone funny?
Walked in with someone else's man?
Tried to get in without paying the cover charge?
Was she WANTED?
All of these questions possessed Steve's mind as he found himself in a room unarmed and surrounded by women. All accusing Eve.
Eve didn't look like she had been hit, but her once beautiful hairstyle was now wildly unkempt. She was yelling and cussing at her attackers.
"What seemed to be the problem?"
Steve questioned as if he was an enforcer of the law, though unarmed. The woman who let him in without charging a cover was the first to speak up.
"Sir?"
She said.
"That woman is not allowed in this club. Not tonight!
Never! Never again. "
The Woman continued.
Steve looked Eve in the eye, piercing through the depths of her drunken soul.

"They don't want you in here, it's obvious. I don't want to see you get shot."

Steve said.

Jeff, her boyfriend, was drunk as a fish and staring at Steve in wonderment. Those guns were retracted.

"Let's get out of here,"

Steve commanded as he led all four passengers back to the car. He later dropped the quartet at Eve's place. Jeff paid for the trip along with a tip. It's been over two decades, and Steve hasn't heard from or seen Eve.

Steve has since become an international bestselling author with some of his content in the moviemaking pipeline.

About The AUTHOR

John Alan Andrews hails from the islands of SVG in the Caribbean. He began his acting career in New York and took his craft to Hollywood in 1996. He appeared in multiple TV Ad campaigns and films, including John Q, starring Denzel Washington. Andrews later found his niche—writing coupled with filmmaking—and not only starred in but produced and directed some of his work, which won multiple awards in Hollywood.

Over 90 books from his multi-genre catalog are in print, including NYC, The Church Series, and Success for Teens. Rude Buay's first novel is poised for a Jamaican production. Andrews is drafting The PIPS—Mediterranean Private Eye Series, a police procedural TV series slated for the Mediterranean enclaves. He has also co-authored several titles with his sons, Jonathan Andrews and Jefferri Andrews.

His latest books, Atomic Steps and Make Every Thought Pay You A Profit, are favorites among business leaders, and his twisted NYC Connivers legal thriller series appeals to both women and men ages 16 -85. The Pips Series (Body in a Suitcase). Also, Samuel A. Andrews—*Legacy* *(A Biography)*.

His work can be found at **ALIPNET.COM** or **ALIPNET TV**, his recently launched OTT Streaming Platform.

John Alan Andrews states: "Some people create, while others compete. Creating is where the rubber meets the road. A dream worth having is one worth fighting for because freedom is not free; it carries a massive price tag."

VISIT: WWW.JOHNAANDREWS.COM

Like Us on Facebook

https://www.facebook.com/Whoshotthesherifffilm

MANY SHADES OF HER

MANY SHADES OF HER

#1 International Bestselling Author
JOHN A. ANDREWS
THE UNTOUCHABLE
RUDE BUAY
An International Secret Service Agent Novel Series...
2

MANY SHADES OF HER

MANY SHADES OF HER

NACIONAL SUPERVENTAS
CHICO RUDO
THE UNSTOPPABLE
EL IMPARABLE
JOHN A. ANDREWS

MANY SHADES OF HER

SAUCE
02:29

A SUSPENSE MYSTERY HORROR
FROM THE CREATOR OF
RUDE BUAY
#1 INTERNATIONAL BESTSELLING AUTHOR
JOHN ALAN ANDREWS

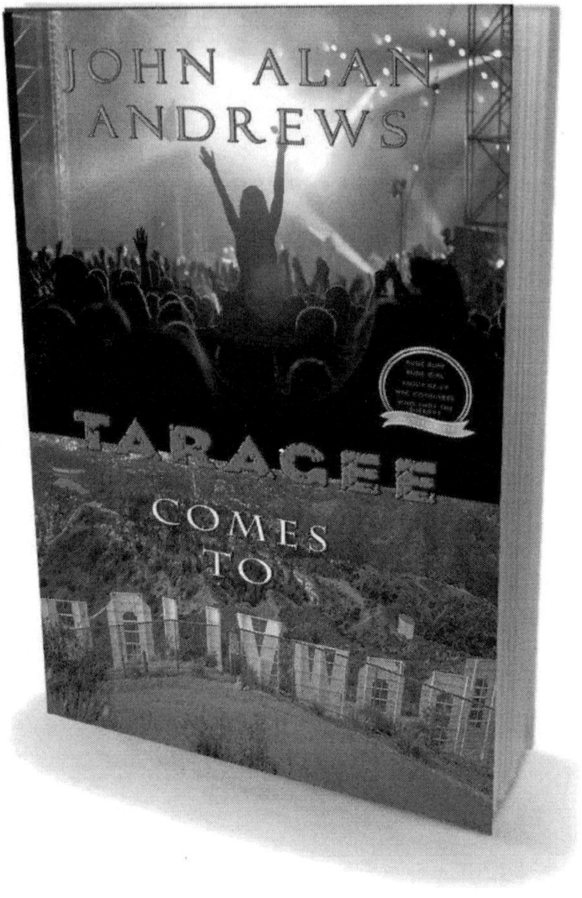
JOHN ALAN
ANDREWS
TARAGEE
COMES
TO

MANY SHADES OF HER

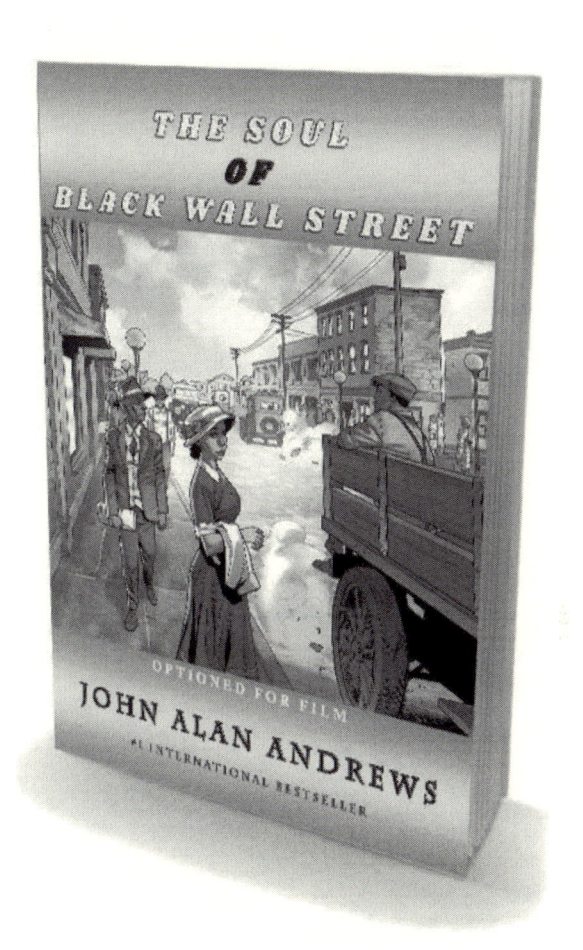

Climbing Up From The Bottom AUTHOR
JOHN A. ANDREWS
Dare To Make A Difference (Success 101)
Spread Some Love (Relationships 101)
The 3 Steps To Changing Your Life
THE SUCCESS TRIANGLE
Three Books In One Volume
Including DARE TO MAKE A DIFFERENCE

MANY SHADES OF HER

ATOMIC STEPS

WIN BIG OR GO HOME

WARNING: If you are determined to stay in your comfort zone, This book may not be for you.

INTERNATIONAL BESTSELLING AUTHOR

JOHN ALAN ANDREWS

MANY SHADES OF HER

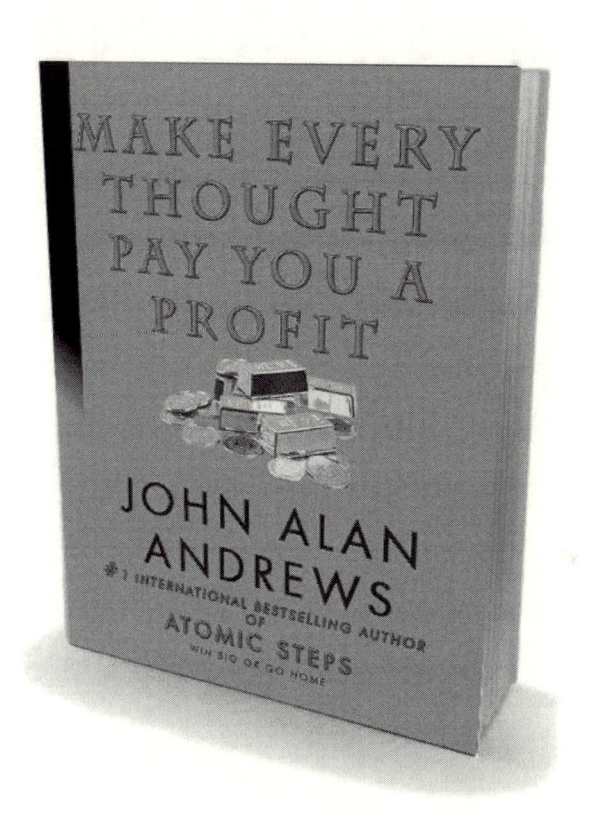

MANY SHADES OF HER

DARE TO MAKE A DIFFERENCE
SUCCESS 101
FOR
ADULTS
#1 INTERNATIONAL BESTSELLING AUTHOR
JOHN A. ANDREWS

MANY SHADES OF HER

MANY SHADES OF HER

DARE TO MAKE A DIFFERENCE
SUCCESS 101
FOR
ADULTS
#1 INTERNATIONAL BESTSELLING AUTHOR
JOHN A. ANDREWS

DARE TO MAKE
A DIFFERENCE
SUCCESS 101
FOR TEENS
JOHN A.
ANDREWS
#1 INTERNATIONAL BESTSELLING AUTHOR

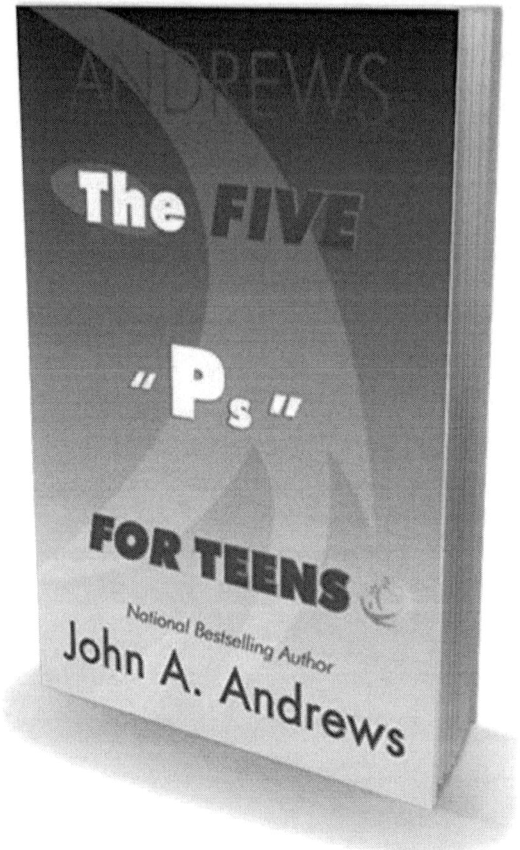
ANDREWS
The FIVE
"Ps"
FOR TEENS
National Bestselling Author
John A. Andrews

ANDREWS
QuoTus
Unlimited
John A. Andrews
Author of
How I Wrote 8-Books-In One Year™

Copyrighted Material
ANDREWS
John A. Andrews
Author of
"Quotes" Unlimited &
How I Wrote 8 Books In One Year™

ECLECTIC
QUOTES
SPEAK WITH
POWER
JOHN A.
ANDREWS
#1 INTERNATIONAL BESTSELLING AUTHOR

MANY SHADES OF HER

THE 5
STEPS TO
CHANGING
YOUR LIFE
BY: JOHN A. ANDREWS
"SEE YOU AT THE SUMMIT"

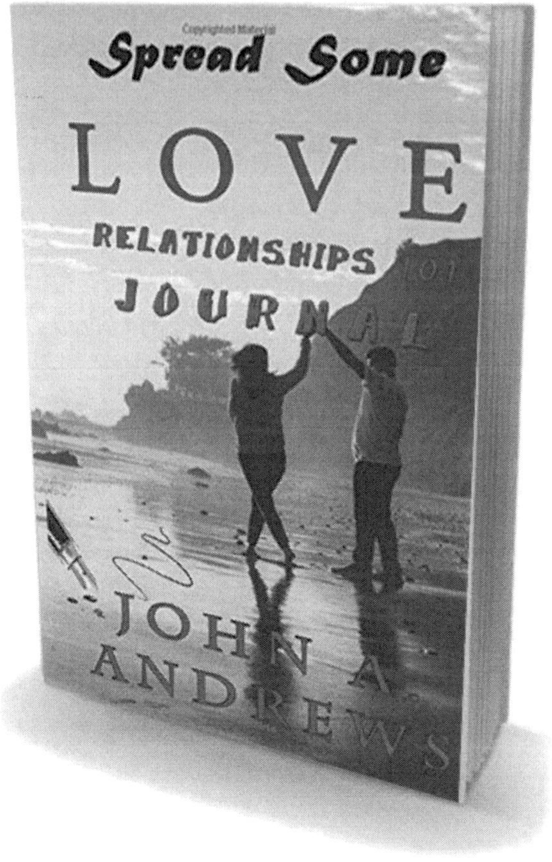
Spread Some
LOVE
RELATIONSHIPS
JOURNAL
JOHN A.
ANDREWS

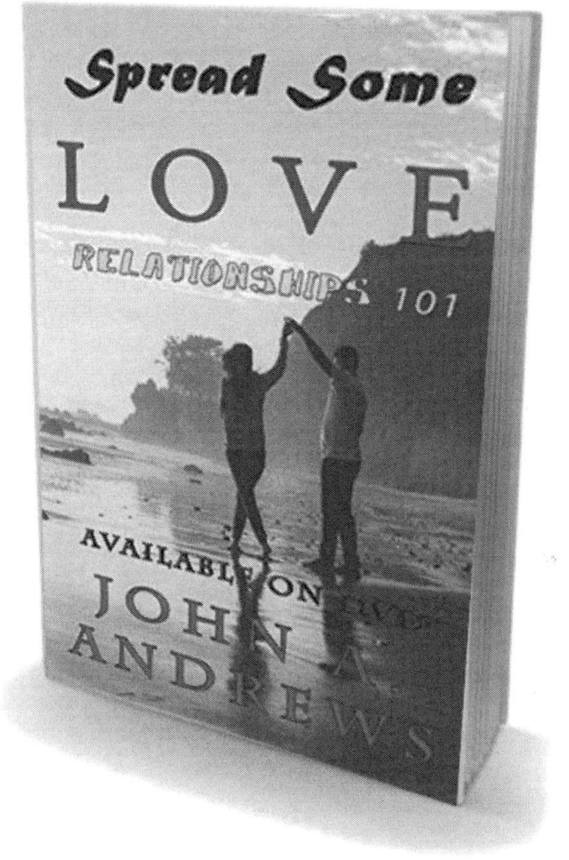
Spread Some
LOVE
RELATIONSHIPS 101
JOHN A.
ANDREWS

MANY SHADES OF HER

MANY SHADES OF HER

MANY SHADES OF HER

MANY SHADES OF HER

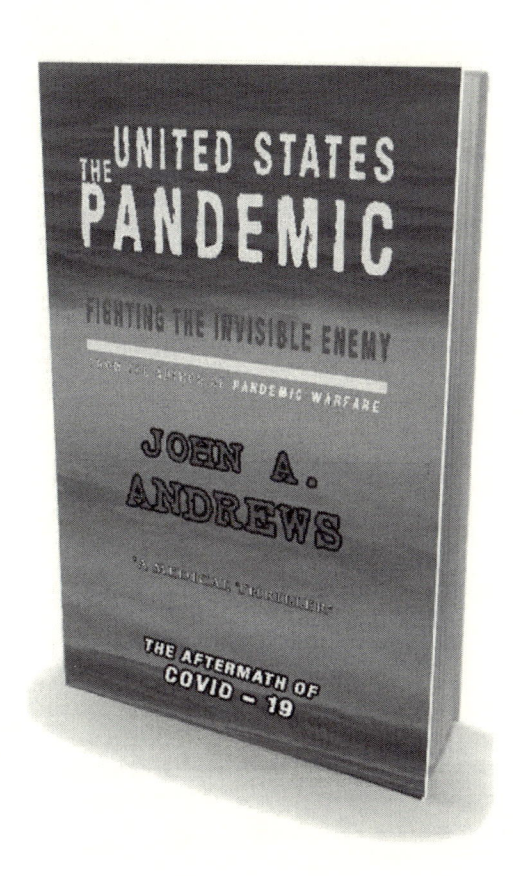

MANY SHADES OF HER

THAT CONNECTS
PRAISE
HEAVEN & EARTH
FROM THE CREATOR OF
THE CHURCH...A HOSPITAL?
JOHN A. ANDREWS
THE
CHURCH
ON FIRE
THE MUSICAL®

MANY SHADES OF HER

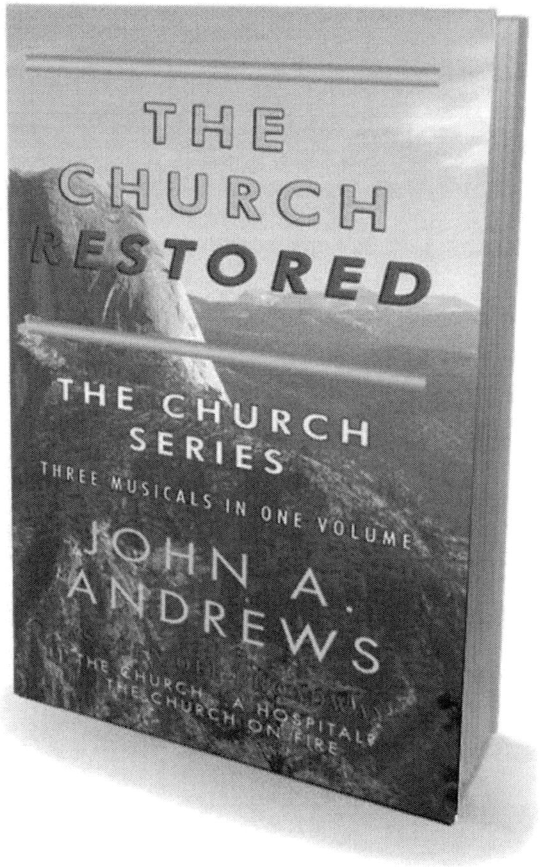
THE CHURCH RESTORED
THE CHURCH SERIES
THREE MUSICALS IN ONE VOLUME
JOHN A. ANDREWS
THE CHURCH... A HOSPITAL?
THE CHURCH ON FIRE

CROSS ATLANTIC FIASCO

A Riveting Novel

THREE EX-COPS, THEIR EX-BOSS, HIS 9 YEAR OLD DAUGHTER, AND THE BIGGEST BANK HEIST EVER ORCHESTRATED...

RENEGADE COPS

#1 INTERNATIONAL BESTSELLER

JOHN A. ANDREWS

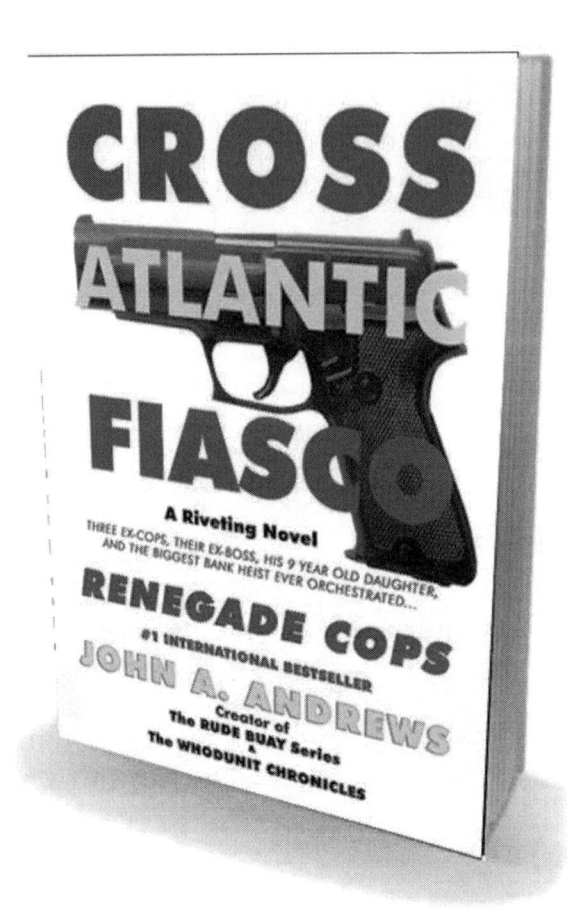

Creator of
The RUDE BUAY Series
&
The WHODUNIT CHRONICLES

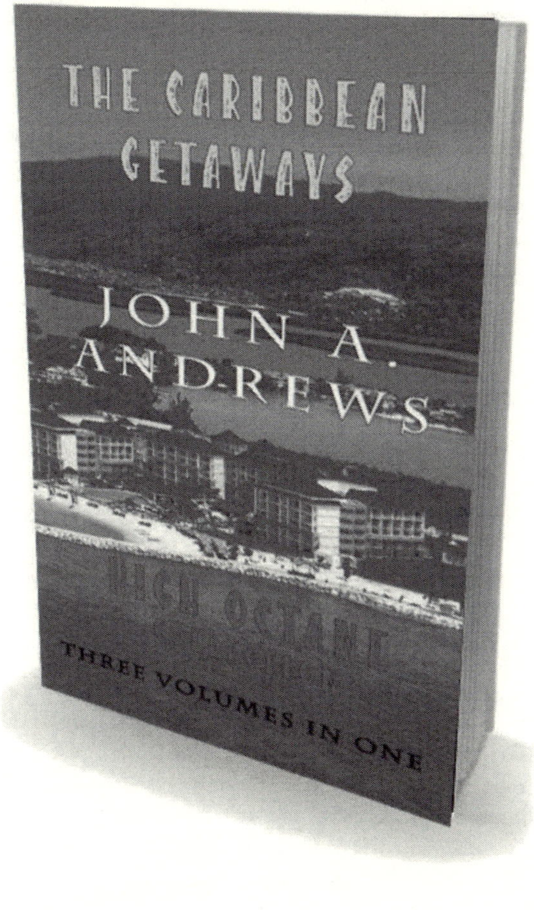
THE CARIBBEAN GETAWAYS
JOHN A. ANDREWS
THREE VOLUMES IN ONE

MANY SHADES OF HER

MANY SHADES OF HER

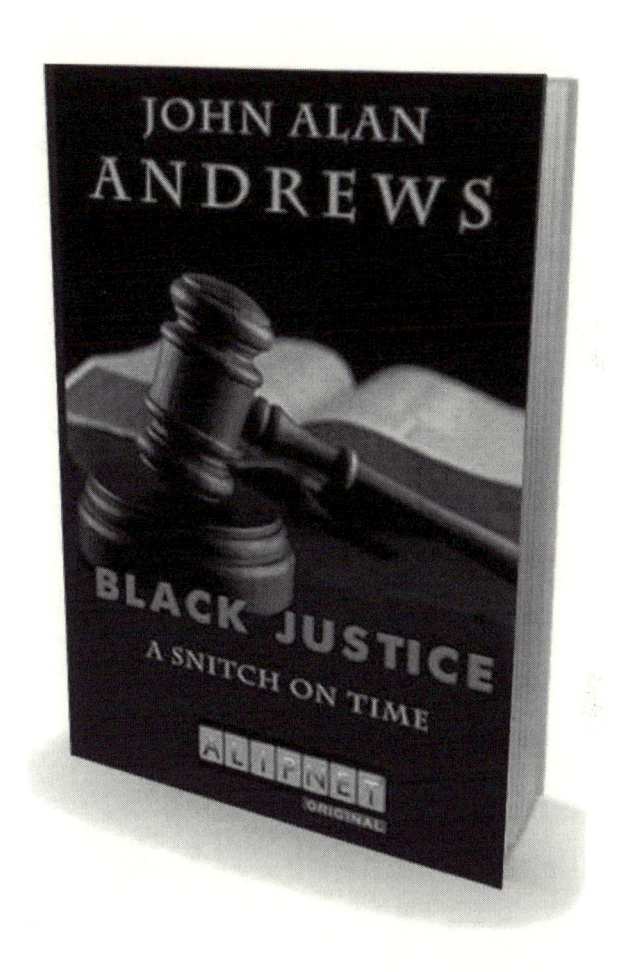

JOHN & JONATHAN
ANDREWS

BLACK JUSTICE
INJUSTICE BAKED IN

MANY SHADES OF HER

CHASING DESTINY

GOT TO HAVE IT!

BASED ON THE NOVEL
A RUDE BUAY SIDEKICK
FROM THE CREATOR OF
RUDE BUAY

JOHN A. ANDREWS

MANY SHADES OF HER

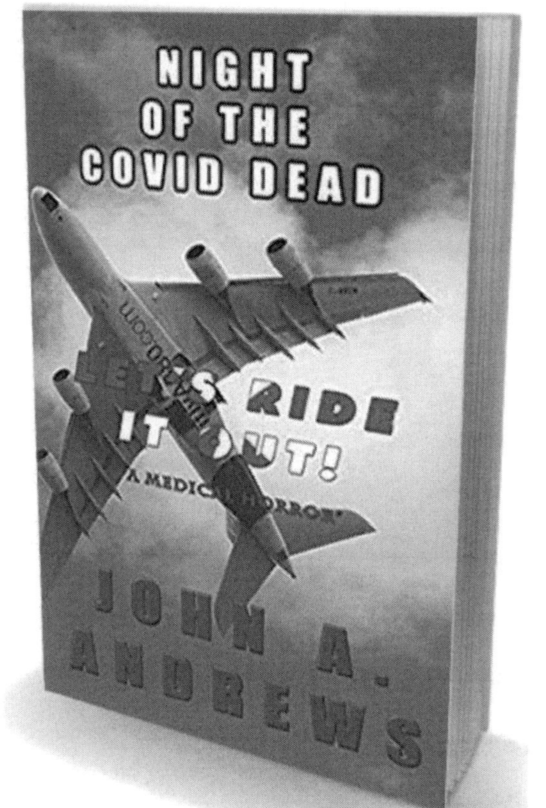
NIGHT
OF THE
COVID DEAD
RIDE
JOHN A.
ANDREWS

THE MACOS
ADVENTURE
REVISED EDITION
A TEEN NOVEL
JONATHAN
&
JEFFERRI
ANDREWS

MANY SHADES OF HER

MANY SHADES OF HER

MANY SHADES OF HER

MANY SHADES OF HER

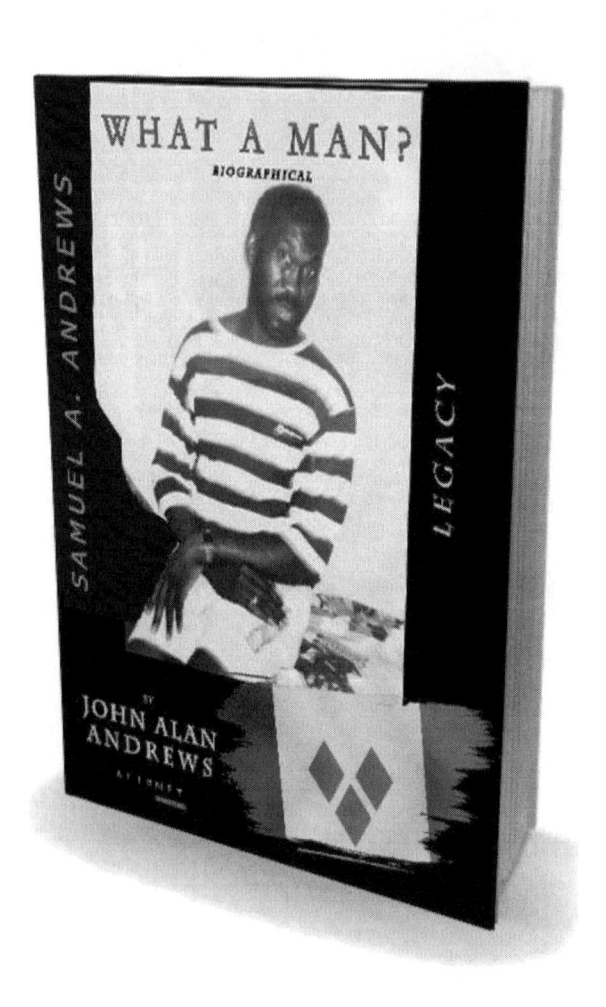

MANY SHADES OF HER

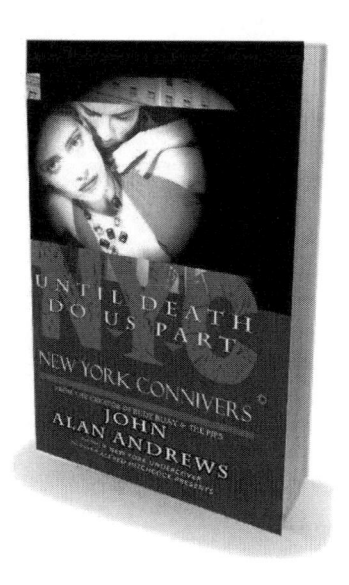

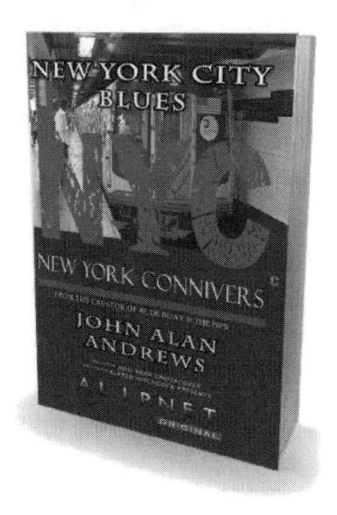

MANY SHADES OF HER

MANY SHADES OF HER

COMING SOON

THE MACOS
ADVENTURE
II
REVISED EDITION
THE AUTHORITY SQUAD
A TEEN NOVEL
JONATHAN
JEFFERRI
&
JOHN
ANDREWS

MANY SHADES OF HER

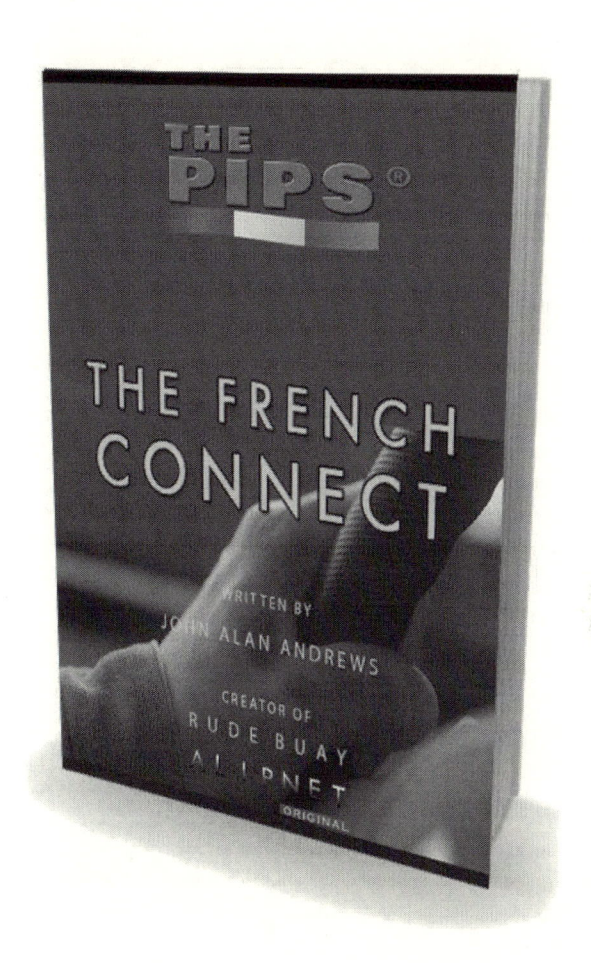

MANY SHADES OF HER

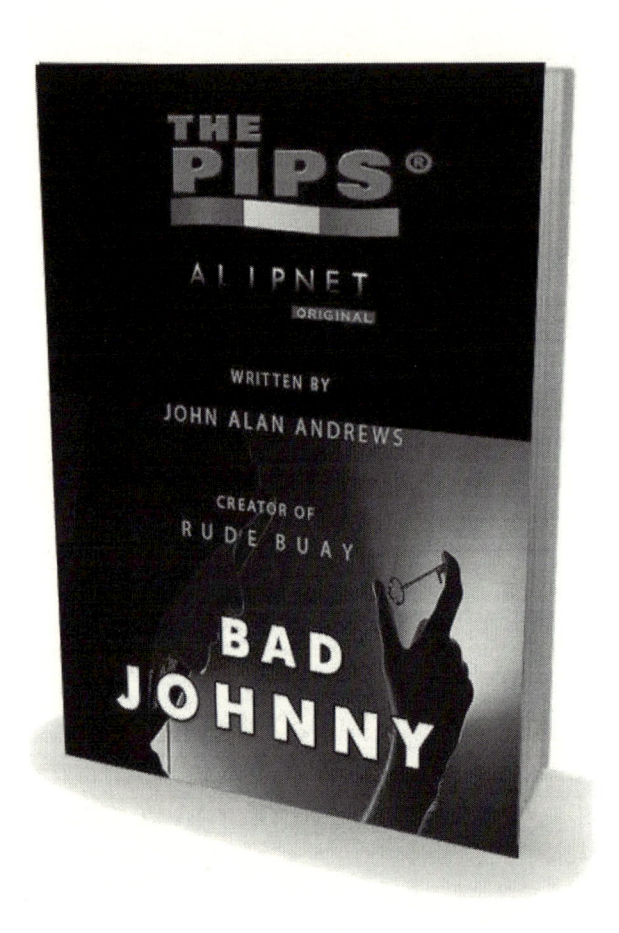

MANY SHADES OF HER

MANY SHADES OF HER

MANY SHADES OF HER

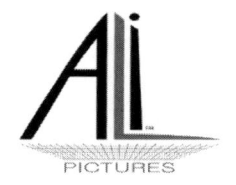

MANY SHADES OF HER

MANY SHADES OF HER

ALIPNET
ORIGINAL

MANY SHADES OF HER